MAELSTROM
PART I

RIP CONVERSE

MAELSTROM
PART I

The characters and events in this book are fictitious. Any similarity to real persons, living or dead, is coincidental and unintended by the author.

1st eBook edition: October 2019

Maelstrom Part I: ISBN 978-1-64669-248-4
Maelstrom Part II: ISBN 978-1-64669-249-1
Maelstrom Part III: ISBN 978-1-64669-250-7
Maelstrom (the whole): ISBN 978-1-64669-251-4

To my father Courtland who died far too young and my mother Joey who lived on; both wonderful people whom I admire greatly.

Many thanks to my wife Louise for cover design, social media, encouragement and emotional support in this my first work, to MH Syin for her help with editing and proofreading and to a small group of beta readers, whose careful reading along the way helped me to complete this work. Thank you all.

Table of Contents

Chapter 1

There is nothing quite so dark and empty as the soul of an alcoholic at four in the morning. More than 10 years had passed since his last drink, but the shapeless waves of guilt and inadequacy that surged through him felt as real and exigent as those from the old days when he would awaken with the sheets beneath him damp and soiled with night sweats. He felt like crawling out of his own skin.

A cool breeze blew in through the cracked window next to the bed, but it provided no relief as the air was super-heated the moment it entered the room by a broken steam radiator located under the window. It answered exclusively to an ancient, insensitive thermostat located in some distant room and could not be turned off. The Congregational Church across the street added to his discomfort. Some years before the church elders had installed a new set of bells and unilaterally decided it was imperative that all residents within a six-block radius be made aware of the time on an hourly basis. This annoyed Ryan more than usual. Knowing the precise time when it turned 2, 3, and finally 4:00 a.m. only served to underscore his inability to sleep.

'Fuckers all probably live on the other side of town,' he thought to himself.

Ryan turned his head toward his numb arm for perhaps the fifth time in as many minutes, dead and useless and swore softly. In his college days they made jokes about "pulling a coyote" in situations like the one he found himself in. When coyotes are caught in a snare, they sometimes chew off their own leg to escape. Despite his pain, Ryan knew moving his arm would risk waking the woman who slept so peacefully atop it, and he toyed with the idea for several seconds.

Ryan was in love with the idea of love. He did loving things, said loving things and made love a lot, but during his 37 years on the planet he had seldom used the 'L' word as in "I love you." except for a few times in high school. It never sounded right coming out of his mouth so

1

he stopped and planned on saving it for *the* love. When he found her and used it, he wanted it to mean something. The concept was sacred to him, and he didn't want to cheapen the word through premature or excessive use.

The woman asleep on his arm was perfectly pleasant to be with, but like a hundred before her, she fell short. The problem was his ideal changed from week to week, sometimes day to day and the character traits he sought were often in direct conflict with one another. Terrified of ending up alone, he kept searching because to not do so would be an admission to a lonely and pointless future. Right now, he wanted out and away from the responsibility of explaining himself and after pondering various options, decided a slow withdrawal of his arm in combination with a feigned rollover as his best one. He held his breath and began the delicate maneuver.

She awoke instantly as if some invisible tether between them had tensed. "Ryan, are you OK?" she moaned sleepily.

"Yes." he answered after a brief pause. "I have to go, but I didn't want to wake you."

"You have to go? Why, what time is it?"

He searched his mind for a plausible excuse that wouldn't hurt or offend yet allow immediate exit. "It's about 4:30 and I have to go because ..." he couldn't think of one. "If I stay here one second longer, I think I might puke."

Fully awake, Michelle reached over to touch his forehead and check for a fever.

"You don't feel well do you?"

He recoiled from her extended hand like a petulant child, tempted to mimic her query. "I need my own bed."

She switched on the bedside table light and turned back to him with that look in her eyes as he pulled on his shirt and pants. She knew, had felt him pulling away for days and anything he said would make the whole thing worse.

"Maybe we should talk."

"No, I have to go."
She looked at him sadly but also knowingly. "Can't we ...?"

"Not now, maybe later." He wanted to get out before her hurt boiled to the surface and the tears started. He became almost frantic as he buttoned his jeans.

She surprised him. "Your loss Ryan," and turned the light out as he rushed from the room. She waited for the stretching sound of the spring on the screen door before allowing herself any tears.

He skipped the steps and leapt off the side of the porch as the door slapped shut behind him and landed in the dewy grass with his shoes in hand. Cold, small beads of moisture sprinkled the tops of his still hot bare feet as he cut across her lawn, reminding him that the first hard frost of fall would arrive any day. "What is wrong with me?" he asked himself. But even as he walked the short distance back to the boatyard he wondered if ending things with Michele had been the right thing to do.

Sippican Village is a quintessential New England town on Cape Cod. It continued to slumber as he walked the two short blocks through the village center. He was glad for his bare feet. The noise of shod feet would have woken at least one dog, which in turn would have woken them all. Sippican had not changed a bit in his 37 years, but he had; enough to finally leave the small town from which he had drawn his sense of self for too long. One day he'd simply woken up and realized that the dreams and values he had pursued and attempted to emulate for half a lifetime were those of his parents and grandparents. There was nothing wrong with them, they simply weren't his.

He passed by the tidy, little Captain's cottages left behind from the whaling days, the general store, post office and the band-concert shell on the village green. Sippican's seduction was easy to understand; carefree and protected, clambakes, fireworks, small-town parades, huge family reunions, tennis, sailing, fishing, yacht club and tennis club dances, not to mention a plethora of attractive, educated and willing young women. What wasn't to like?

He walked into the dark boatyard. It was starting to fill up with all the boats that would be stored ashore for winter. They were scattered about in varying states of readiness for the coming snow and freezing temperatures. Some were still rigged with their masts in. Others had been stripped of their rigging and now had crude frames of fir strapping material built onto their decks. These appeared almost skeletal in the predawn light. Once the frames were complete, giant sheets of shrink-wrap would be applied to keep out the winter snow and ice. He kept thinking about Michelle but felt as though the relationship was depleted ground that he'd plowed over far too many times. What was the point? He would be gone soon. It was early October and he planned to be out of the boatyard headed South on his sailboat Parthenia in four to six weeks' time. By then the hurricane season would have passed, but it would still be early enough to avoid most of the cold, unpredictable weather of late fall on the first leg of his trip to Bermuda.

Ryan rounded the corner of the shed where Parthenia stood on poppet stands and was startled as a huge, black shape rose out of the dirt, snorted several times, and bound out at him from the dark shed.

"Clifton! You scared the shit out of me!" Ryan squatted down to return the shameless display of affection being offered. Clifton was a four-year-old black Labrador of unusually large stature and minimal grace who was completely devoted to him. The dog was not a brain trust, but his short memory and immeasurable enthusiasm were always welcome and frequently comical. Time meant absolutely nothing to him and whether Ryan left for a week or only 10 minutes, each reunion warranted an effusive, rough, wet welcome.

Ryan turned on the overhead florescent lights and took a moment to stare lovingly at Parthenia. He had acquired the boat almost six years ago, but it was only in the last three months that he'd mustered the courage to sell his house and move onto the boat full time. His decision was based in part on a threatened IRS lien for taxes owed. In the end, he had chosen the boat over the house. He could always buy another house, but they weren't building wooden boats like Parthenia anymore. Built 65 years earlier, she was a wooden, 42-foot, full keel, mahogany sloop

4

designed by Sparkman and Stevens and built in Norway of 1-inch edge glued mahogany planking, fastened over bronze strapped oak frames. She was ideally suited to the ocean travel he loved so much; fast, strong, and stable in the worst weather conditions.

He gave Clifton another quick rubdown before climbing the ladder up onto the deck, then went below to make his first pot of coffee and a work list for the day. He sat at the chart table and critically examined the main cabin while waiting for his coffee to drip through. Messy with tools and sawdust, the cabin had an unmistakable patina that reflected the many sea miles she'd traveled. Every nick, dent and repair in the solid mahogany interior told a story of a race, a crossing, or a difficult trip. Parthenia was like a worn saddle or a favorite pair of jeans and was finally back together again after being torn apart to accommodate the removal and subsequent replacement of her old diesel engine. She'd always been a bit under-powered. With the new engine he expected she would be able to cruise comfortably at 8 knots under power.

It was 6 a.m. by the time he'd changed into work clothes, had his coffee and finished his work list. He hoped to get in several hours of work before the boatyard workers came in and the distractions of the day began. Still dark under the boat where he would be working, he set up several aluminum clip-on lights around the perimeter of the hull and got out the various tools he needed. The hull planks covering Parthenia's frames had all been edge glued with a first-generation epoxy when she was originally built and some of the glue joints were starting to fail, allowing the planks to shrink apart. His solution was to rout out the old epoxy along the joints and to insert splines with modern epoxy. The splines he planned on putting in were of varying lengths, the longest almost 20 feet long. Each was 1/8- to 1/4-inch wide and he would set them into routed channels 3/4-inch deep that ran fore and aft and into the glue joint between all the planks. The skill in replacing them was to cut a new, straight channel that would both remove the old glue line and exactly follow the contour of each of the shaped planks that ran the length of the hull. He adjusted the batten he was using as a guide, placed the high-speed tool up against the hull, plunged the router and started his first cut of the morning. The router spun at 25,000 rpm and the sharp bit cut easily into the wood. Quickly he was covered in fine, aromatic,

African mahogany dust as he ran the tool down the hull. Each of the old planks had been cut from first-cut trees over 300 years old. The smell and texture of the newly exposed wood was rich and exotic like the jungles from which it had been harvested. The first cut went well, and he moved around the hull for the next several hours oblivious to the rest of the world until he felt his knee nudged aggressively from behind.

He knew who it was without looking and turned off the router before looking down into Clifton's big brown eyes. The dog stood stolid and square, tail slowly wagging, looking anxiously back and forth between Ryan's face and a space at his feet where he had dropped a piece of scrap wood. He sensed an opening for play and nudged him again and wagged his tail in a wider arc.

"You really need to get a life."

Clifton's 5-pound tail wagged in a wider arc in response to Ryan's attention and it began to look as though the tail was wagging him.

Ryan laughed out loud. "All right, I get it!" He looked at his watch, surprised to see that almost five hours had passed since he'd started working. He turned off the router, rested it on the staging behind him and blew himself off with the air hose at his feet. Then he smiled down at Clifton, walked over to the workbench, got a tennis ball off the shelf and walked out of the shed towards the beach. Once there he threw the ball for almost 10 minutes up and down the beach until Clifton ran out of gas and lay down at his feet breathing hard. The ball, encrusted with thick saliva and sand, sat safely between his paws. Ryan gave him a moment to rest then continued walking down the beach to the short pier that ran out into the harbor. Clifton followed him with his eyes for a minute and then carefully picked up the ball, dropped it into the water at the ocean's edge, and rinsed it off before picking it back up and following him out onto the pier.

Ryan sat down on a bench at the end, and absently gazed out over the quiet anchorage. Normally full of sailboats in the summer, only a dozen or so remained in the water. The colorful summer mooring balls were being replaced with uniform winter-sticks that made it more difficult for winter ice to carry away the ground tackle laying on the bottom. He watched for several minutes as a solitary boatyard employee on a small work barge changed out another one several hundred yards off the shore. The sun on his face felt good.

Moments later he watched as a large powerboat rounded the entrance buoy at the head of the harbor. It stood out because it was huge, over 120-feet long, the kind of yacht one would normally see in Palm Beach or on the Riviera and seldom in small, sleepy villages like Sippican. Ryan figured the owner had paid at least $20 million or $30 million for it and he was curious what such a person would be doing in their small town at this time of year. The small, high-speed Cigarette launch cradled on its upper, aft-deck cost as much as his boat, and he stood watching for a few more minutes as the ship anchored in the deeper water at the harbor entrance. The captain of the vessel steered from the wings of the bridge and was communicating with two of his crew on the bow by radio. When the ship finally came head to wind and stopped, one of the crew tripped the brake on the windlass and a large Danforth anchor dropped from the bow cavity on the port side. Thick, half-inch chain followed the anchor towards the bottom and made a loud, distinctive *chunka, chunka, chunka* sound as the individual links ran over and through the bow chalk. The sound was clearly audible from half mile away.

Ryan thought about the cost of operating such a vessel. The rule of thumb was that operating costs for any vessel are approximately 15 percent of the original purchase price, every year. He did some quick math in his head and figured annual maintenance and crew expenses for the yacht to be over $3,000,000/year; a staggering sum in his simple world. He shook his head and then looked at his watch and decided to take an early lunch.

His small inflatable Zodiac was tied at the float below he got up off the bench and started walking down the gangway. Clifton knew right away what going down to the lower float meant and raced ahead and bounded into their small outboard. Ryan started the engine and after untying the bow line they idled away from the dock and started motoring in the general direction of The Black Watch restaurant across the harbor. Clifton stood, legs apart in the bow, taking up half the length of the small inflatable and savored the breeze through his jowls. Ryan angled his course a few degrees to get a closer look at the powerboat. As they got closer, he watched as the crew of the yacht launched the Cigarette and prepared to get the smaller boat underway. Once it was in the water one of the crew climbed down into it and started the powerful racing engines. They idled with a distinctive, angry, staccato sound that he could easily hear over the sound of his small outboard. Two other passengers got on board, they dropped their lines and the operator slammed the throttles forward, emitting an obnoxious blatting sound as the propellers sought purchase. They came up on a plane and did a tight circle around the mother ship before straightening out and heading towards the town landing. They clearly had no intention of observing the no wake, 5 mph speed zone and quickly accelerated to 30 or 40 knots.

Ryan realized they were going to cross his bow quite closely and changed his course to give them more berth. He expected them to slow as they neared, out of courtesy, but that didn't happen. Instead of slowing down and veering away they turned directly towards him and only at the last possible second, before hitting him, turned away; throwing wake and spray directly into his tiny Zodiac. He saw what was going to happen and cut his throttle and hung onto both sides of his boat with his weight low in the bottom. Clifton lacked his insight into fluid dynamics, however, and when the wake hit them, was thrown into the water.

"You fucking asshole!" Ryan screamed at their stern. The operator didn't stop and instead laughed and pounded the dashboard in amusement as he looked backward over his shoulder. He was deeply tanned and had a ponytail.

Ryan struggled to pull Clifton's slippery, wet body back into the boat and promised himself a confrontation with the driver if an opportunity presented itself. The man had no business operating a boat, and he imprinted the faces of the operator and his two associates into his mind. Clifton of course didn't care that he got wet, but Ryan did. The seawater temperature was in the low fifties already and in the process of pulling Clifton back aboard, his pants and sweater had gotten soaked. Ryan was furious. He pulled the drain plug in the stern of the Zodiac to let the seawater out and after getting back underway, set a course close enough to the yacht to see its name and registry. 'White Lady' was written across her stern in big gold letters, under that, 'Grand Cayman.' The vessel was definitely white, but he wondered if the name didn't have another meaning? It was also of Cayman Registry which was one of the biggest offshore tax havens for illegal money. Once he reached the other side of the harbor, Ryan tied off his dinghy and walked into The Black Watch. He was still fuming as he sat down at the bar.

***

Tory McCane was just 1,000 feet away from The Black Watch restaurant. She had pulled over to the side of the road to enter an address in her GPS. Her two children were hungry and running out of patience. They'd been driving since seven that morning. Tory's 12-year-old daughter Jan sat in the front seat next to her. Her 5-year-old son Willy sat in the back.

"Mum, that's the third time you've put that same address in the GPS. Obviously, it's not in the data base. We're going to have to ask someone for directions," Jan said.

"Not in the data-base? What does that even mean? It's a real street for God's sake. Rick and Stephanie have lived there for 6 years!"

"But obviously Google doesn't know that. Garbage in, garbage out. You know, when you do the same thing over and over expecting different results it's called insanity."

"Where did I get you kids?"

"You had us through a normal birth process."

"Well you sound like aliens sometimes. Okay, next person or place I see I'll ask directions."

Willy gave Jan's hair a tug from the back seat.

"Hey shrimp, cut that out or I'll come back there and give you an Indian burn or a wedgie you'll never forget."

"Kids, come on. We're almost there."

Tory was annoyed, but not with her kids. It was mainly because she couldn't find her friend's house. Between the treatment center and the halfway house afterward, Tory had been separated from her children for almost a year and it was all she could do not to pull over every five seconds and simply hug them both. They were good kids. It was a miracle that she hadn't totally messed them up with her years of substance abuse and frequent absences. She was certain it was all behind her now and was determined to build a solid new life for the three of them. Her husband Will had bailed on them right after Willy's birth and the divorce papers arrived several weeks later. She'd agreed to a quick divorce in exchange for a one-time cash payment, but as part of that deal had forfeited ongoing child support. That had been a mistake. Her drug and alcohol use had gotten completely out of control as she'd struggled to take care of the two of them as a single parent. Once she was fully into the drugs and alcohol, she quickly burned through the rest of her divorce settlement and they'd lived hand-to-mouth much of the time. Her relationship with Will was the last relationship she'd been in.

"Mum, there's a restaurant up ahead. Let's ask directions there."

***

Phil snickered as Ryan sat down at the bar. "Did you and Clifton run into an unexpected storm?"

"Funny Phil, did you see those assholes in the Cigarette?"

"Yeah, as a matter of fact I did. Seemed like a couple of rich jerks. You want the regular?"

Ryan nodded. Phil was the owner, bartender and cook at The Black Watch. He squirted soda water over ice and then added a splash of Rose's lime juice to the glass and set it in front of Ryan. Then he reached into a jar on the bar-top for a piece of pickled sausage and flipped it to Clifton who was politely standing at attention under the waitress station waiting for the treat and wolfed it down.

"Jesus Phil, I wish you wouldn't give him those damn things. They make him fart something terrible."

"I know, but he likes it and I can't refuse the big Cliff anything. Look at the mug on this dog, he's got to be the biggest stud in town." He flipped up the station top and knelt to pat Clifton's big wet head as the lab chewed up the savory treat.

"You know Ryan, I shouldn't let him in here. The Board of Health would take my license if they saw him in here."

"Phil, I seriously doubt the health inspector has even been in this dive. If he had you'd already be shut down. If he ever does come in here, just tell him I'm socially handicapped and that he's a service dog and helps me get into meaningful contact with other human beings."

"Yeah, right! This 'canine specimen' is nothing but a chowhound and you are nothing but a pussy-hound." He gave Clifton a last pat on the head and stood up.

"So, are you going to have some lunch today or is this just a beverage stop? The special is fried calamari in garlic, onions and those sweet/hot Portuguese peppers you like."

"Sounds good to me." Ryan sat back to sip his soda water while Phil went off to the kitchen to prepare the meal. The only other people in the bar were a quiet threesome playing pool in the other room and Smitty, a retired auto body man. Between a lifetime of paint and solvent fumes and the quart of vodka he drank each day, Smitty wasn't quite 'there' anymore. He was taking a nap on the other side of the bar. Ryan was reflective for a moment. He'd been a lot like Smitty back in the day and almost died of all the alcohol he'd consumed until a cousin introduced him to AA. He'd talked to Smitty several times about maybe hitting a meeting with him and trying to get off the sauce, but he was in the late stages of alcoholism and Ryan doubted he had a recovery in him. Lost in his thoughts for the moment he didn't hear the door open and was startled when he heard a female voice address him from behind.

"Hey, is this dog vicious?"

Ryan turned at the sound of the voice and stared at the speaker without replying right away. She met his stare and cocked her head to one side.

"Hello? Anybody home?"

"I'm sorry, I didn't mean to stare. No, he's not vicious at all unless you're allergic to dog saliva."

The woman was extraordinarily attractive and had a refreshing directness about her. Standing behind and close to her side were two children. Clifton loved children and hearing them come in had rushed over to greet them. Their reaction to his size and quick movement in their direction was predictable and quite prudent.

"Thanks, I wanted to be sure. The kids are a little frightened of big dogs and this fellow is, well, … large!"

Clifton started to rub his head against the little girl's leg. She appeared to be about twelve; her brother five or six. She was tentatively petting his head, and everyone seemed to relax. Ryan couldn't stop staring at the woman. She looked to be in her late 20s, petite with blue eyes, about 5-foot-3, slender and had long curly blond hair. She projected a powerful, confident life force. The two children were also very attractive and similar in appearance.

"Do you work here?"

"No, I'm a customer, in for a bite of lunch and some friendly conversation."

She looked around the bar wondering who there was to converse with. "With him?" she nodded towards Smitty who had his head on his arms and was snoring loudly across the bar.

Ryan laughed. "No, Smitty over there is busy looking for holes on the inside of his eyelids. I talk to Phil when he's not in the kitchen cooking and sometimes myself. My name's Ryan, Ryan Cunningham."

"Hi Ryan, I'm Tory McCane and these are my two kids Willy and Jan."

"Nice to meet you all. You here for lunch?"

"No, we're looking for Mary Celeste Road. We have friends who live there, but my GPS doesn't seem to think it exists."

"Well that's easy, Mary Celeste Road is on the other side of the harbor. When you leave the parking lot turn right, follow Water Street around the shoreline to the other side. Turn right onto South Street and Mary Celeste Road will be your first left off that. I'd offer to show you myself, but I came by outboard boat and my lunch should be out any minute."

Both children were now giggling and wrestling with Clifton in the middle of the floor. He was lying on his back flopping his ungainly body from side to side hoping one of them would rub his stomach. Tory and Ryan watched for a moment without saying anything, enjoying the sight.

"He seems like a love."

"He is," Ryan agreed.

Willy stood up from the floor noticing Ryan looking at them.

"Hey mister, want to see me stand on one foot for a full 10 seconds?"

Ryan smiled. "Yes, indeed I would. I don't think I've seen anyone stand on one foot in years. That would of course be unassisted and not touching anything with your hands."

Willy spread his arms out to the side, poked his tongue between his lips, and closed his eyes for several seconds before lifting one leg off the floor and holding it there.

"Mum, time me."

He lasted five seconds before wobbling and dropping his raised leg to keep from falling over.

"Wait, wait, that didn't count. I was just warming up. Mum, do the time again!"

Tory smiled at Ryan and then pointedly looked down at her wrist again.

"Okay, go."

Willy raised his leg again and Ryan and Tory both watched. He made it on the second try.

"Okay, ... time!" Tory shouted.

Ryan politely clapped. "Pretty amazing Willy. I don't think I could do that."

Willy smiled from ear to ear as he looked up at Ryan. He held out his hand.

"What?" Ryan asked.

"You owe me a buck."

"Say what! You never told me that part of the trick."

Ryan turned to Tory. "Your kid's a goddamn con-artist!"

"Goddamn. That's another 50 cents." Willy added.

"What're you talking about?"

"I get paid for swear words too. 'Goddamn' is a 50-cent word."

Tory looked down at Willy. "Maybe this time you can let the nice man slide on the fees and penalties. After all, we just met him. We don't want to scare him off."

"No, that's okay." Ryan pulled out his wallet and took out a dollar bill and handed it to him.

"Next time I'll be more careful around you. You're quite an entrepreneur."

"Ryan, you don't have to give him anything. He's always pulling stunts like that." Tory offered.

"It's okay, I like his spirit." Ryan passed the bill down to Willy who snatched it out of his hand. Willy turned to his sister with a big smile on his face and did a little victory fist pump like he'd just sunk a 20-foot putt.

"Well, come on kids, we've got to get going." She turned to Ryan and smiled pleasantly. "Thanks, you've been helpful. Sorry you got taken by my kid."

"Well, you're welcome. It's a small town, maybe I'll run into you again," he said hopefully. "I live right down in the area you're headed, on my sailboat, at the boatyard."

"What's her name?"

"Parthenia. She's a 42-foot wooden sloop in shed number 2."

"Maybe." Tory smiled looking him in the eye, then turned to her two children. "Come on you two, let's go."

Ryan and Clifton sat staring after them as they left, both with their mouths open and equally disappointed that they hadn't stayed longer. A few moments later Phil returned from the kitchen with Ryan's calamari. He gazed around the room as he set down the plate.

"Did I miss something? I could have sworn I heard someone come in."

"Oh, not much, unless you're into goddesses," Ryan relayed.

"You're kidding, right?"

Ryan took on a wistful expression. "I'm not sure."

"Christ, you're always falling in love. What did she want?"

"She was looking for Mary Celeste Road and I graciously took time out of my busy day to assist her."

"What, you're really going to do something this afternoon? Won't that interfere with your nap?"

"Funny Phil."

Ryan tucked into the fried calamari. It was delicious. Hot, sweet, and buttery it was coated with a perfect crispy breading. After a quick cup of coffee, he paid Phil for the lunch and headed back to the boatyard to finish the spline gluing. As he idled the Zodiac by the town landing, he noted that the Cigarette was still tied up there and again pondered what interest they could have in their little town.

He finished for the day at 5:30 p.m. and after showering and changing in the marina showers, walked back to the boat and fed Clifton. While he ate, Ryan walked around the perimeter of Parthenia, admiring his work, poking and feeling for the dryness of the epoxy and thought about where he would eat dinner. He decided on a small country inn called Laura's that he occasionally frequented about 15 minutes out of town. Before leaving, he knelt and gently scratched Clifton behind the ears as he finished the few remaining scraps in his bowl. The dog predictably started wagging his tail and turned to rub his head (and food encrusted jowls) on Ryan's clean white shirt.

"Oh no you don't you slob," Ryan laughed and ran the short distance to his truck with Clifton loping behind. Ryan got there first and opened the tailgate so Clifton could jump in and the two left for the brief ride to the restaurant. When they pulled into the parking lot at Laura's Ryan noted a black limousine with tinted windows parked out front. The nearest limo rental company he knew of was at least 20 miles away and he was curious who would rent a limousine to come this distance to an out-of-the-way restaurant like Laura's. He entered the small country inn and was greeted by the owner.

"Ryan, how're you? You haven't been by in ages!"

"I'm fine Laura, I felt like giving myself a little treat tonight and I couldn't think of a better place."

"Where's Michelle?"

Ryan shrugged. "I guess Michelle is well…. wherever Michelle is."

Laura rolled her eyes. "What, did you two have a fight again?"

"No, I think it went beyond that this time. Got any cute girlfriends?"

Ryan and Laura had been friends since childhood and had even been lovers for a brief period about 12 years before. She'd known him at his worst and was as independent as him. Although their fling hadn't lasted long, they'd remained good friends.

"Well, I won't probe. I can probably guess what happened between you two."

Ryan changed the subject. "Will you join me for dinner?"

15

"I can't, I'm down a hostess tonight and have to greet people as they come in. If you don't mind me getting up all the time, I'll have a drink and an appetizer with you."

"I'd like that."

They sat in the small outer dining room next to the wood stove. "How's that adorable hound of yours?"

"He's fine, waiting patiently in the truck." As he sipped his drink Ryan ran his eyes around the main dining room looking for familiar faces and did a double take. "Ponytail," his two associates and a fourth man whom Ryan didn't recognize were seated on the far side of the room having dinner.

"Do you know those guys?" He motioned with his head to their table.

Laura followed his gaze. "No, I don't think so. They showed up in that limousine parked out front about an hour ago. Why, should I?"

"No, I suppose not. They arrived this afternoon in a mega-yacht and almost drowned Clifton and me as we crossed the harbor. They were on their way into the town landing in one of those high-speed Cigarettes and thought it would be amusing to see how close they could come to us at 30 or 40 knots. Clifton got thrown out of the boat and they damn near swamped me with their wake. I'd like to teach the asshole with the ponytail some manners."

Laura stared at him for a moment before replying. She knew Ryan to have a long fuse and had only seen him lose it once before, but she could tell he was close by the intensity of his expression.

"Ryan, do me a favor and wait until they leave. I don't want a scene here in the restaurant."

Her concern brought him back to reality.

"I'm sorry Laura, of course."

His comment about teaching them some manners was misleading as it suggested a casual familiarity with violence, a trait that Ryan did not, in fact possess. He wasn't particularly fearful of bodily injury and had spent several years studying martial arts, but he cherished his sobriety of 10 years and knew that those few times in his past when he'd lost control and committed violent acts against others left him with a deep sense of sadness and shame which only brought him closer to a drink. It simply wasn't a part of his sober nature and he suddenly felt like an ass for his tough comment and tried to return his attention to Laura and the promised meal. He ordered a grilled radicchio salad with hot goat cheese and crab cakes with pistachio butter. It was good to catch up with her and after a few minutes he was able to relax and enjoy his food. Whenever she got up to seat other diners, he found his thoughts returning to the woman that he'd given directions to earlier in the day. She really was beautiful and the combination of energy and independence that he'd sensed in her had made an impression. He hoped he would run into her again.

The people from the yacht got louder and more boisterous as their meal progressed and it became increasingly difficult to ignore them. Ryan and Laura had both noticed that the man Ryan had nicknamed "Ponytail" was giving the waitress a hard time. Each time she passed near him he would try to fondle her ass. Not in the crass way of a simple drunk, but as if he owned her, and they knew each other well. Jean, the waitress, handled his unwanted attentions without making a fuss, but Ryan could tell she was becoming flustered. She'd spent a lot of time serving the table and was not anxious to lose her tip, so simply avoided his side of the table after a while. During the meal Ryan noticed the man with the ponytail made several trips to the men's room and each time he returned, he was more outgoing and ebullient. Ryan guessed he was doing coke. Eventually, the man made the connection that Jean was purposefully avoiding his side of the table and, biding his time, waited until she passed near enough to clear his plate. He reached out and pinched her, hard, on the back of the leg. Jean dropped her tray and cried out in genuine pain. He looked up at her like she was a piece of meat.
"I don't appreciate being ignored."
Ryan and Laura both jumped up from their table and headed into the dining room to confront him. He didn't see them coming as his back was to the smaller room, but his associates did and were immediately on either side of him, facing Ryan down.

17

Jean was crying, more from the humiliation of the situation than anything else. Ryan's demeanor was cold and purposeful as he approached their table.

The fourth person at the table stood and said to Ponytail, "Edward, I don't want any trouble here. Do you hear me?"

Ryan pulled up short of the associates who'd assumed the stance of bodyguards, positioning themselves between him and Edward.
"Edward, so that's your name. You're an asshole Eddie. You're also a bully. Why don't you tell your boys here to have a seat and the two of us will go outside and I'll give you a few etiquette lessons," Ryan said.

The fourth man interrupted again. "Edward, if you attract any more attention our business will be done. We've spoken about this before. The people I work for frown on public displays like this. Am I being clear?"

Edward had not yet spoken, but it was clear from his tense and coiled body language that he would like nothing better than to beat the piss out of Ryan. But he was also paying attention to the fourth man, and after a tense pause where it could have gone either way he spoke. "Of course, Mr. Slade, no problem."

The man called Slade then turned to Laura.
"I apologize for my friend's behavior, it was inexcusable. We've finished our meal and I think it best that we leave." He pulled out his wallet and placed several-hundred-dollar bills on the table. "The food was delicious. Again, please accept my apologies and give what remains to the waitress who was offended."
Ryan still wanted to have a go at Edward, but that was not going to be possible with the two goons between him and their boss as everyone put on their coats and started to leave. Ryan and Laura followed the four of them to the door.

Edward turned back to Ryan. "I thought I recognized you. You're the guy in the dinghy with the big black dog I saw earlier today. Perhaps we will run into one another again. By the way, you really should learn to drive better or get a bigger boat."

"You fucking asshole." Ryan boiled over and started for him. Laura jumped between them and held Ryan back by pushing on his chest.

"Ryan, let it go."

"Yes Ryan, let it go," Edward suggested, gave a final laugh and disappeared out the door.

"What an idiot! Why'd you stop me?" Ryan started to go around Laura to follow them out to the parking lot.

"For Christ's sake, don't be stupid! There are four of them!"

Ryan was shaking he was so angry. He knew she was right and that things would almost certainly turn out poorly for him if he acted on his anger. He kicked a chair in frustration. "I'm sorry Laura. I don't know what I was thinking."

"Believe me, I understand your anger at the guy, but I don't want you to get hurt or turn my lovely restaurant into a fight club!"

"I know. Listen, I've got to get out of here and cool off. How much do I owe you?"

"Don't worry about it, just take me out to dinner some night before you leave on your trip and we'll call it square."

"I'd like that."

Laura wasn't quite convinced that he had given up the idea of going after the men. "Ryan, are you sure you're all right? I can leave early, and we can go back to my place or something."

"Thanks, I'll be fine, I just had a little temporary insanity and I think it's passed. But I'll take you up on your offer another time." He reached out and touched her arm and then added a lecherous smile to reassure her.

Laura smiled back and then hit him on the arm. "That's not what I meant!"

As Ryan walked across the parking lot, he figuratively kicked himself for letting such a dirtball get under his skin. He knew from experience that whenever he let his ego make decisions he was headed for trouble and that the best medicine would be an AA meeting. He looked at his watch and realized that he still had time to get to one at a small Methodist church several minutes away. He hadn't been to a meeting in several weeks but his behavior at Laura's underscored that he couldn't get away from them altogether without risking his sobriety.

The meeting had already started when he got there, and he took a seat near the back of the room so as not to disturb the speaker. He started to cool down right away. Surrounded by his kind of people, most of the day's anxiety slid away and was replaced by the gathered strength, hope and peace of those in the room. People from all walks of life and economic backgrounds all working to stay away from alcohol. Ryan got caught up in the similarities between himself and the speaker. Toward the end of their respective drinking careers both had been round-the-clock drinkers whose entire lives revolved around the bottle. All waking energy was devoted to getting the drink, drinking the drink, sleeping off a drunk or trying to get out of the trouble that alcohol brought them. Each had also settled for second best in every aspect of their lives including work, relationships and family. Everything had taken a backseat to drinking. In Ryan's case, cocaine had also played a part in his eventual downfall, but AA made little distinction between drugs as it was their opinion that they were all bad if you had an addictive personality and once you were ready to give up, they all had to go.

As the first speaker concluded and went back to his seat, Ryan looked around the room. He was both surprised and pleased to see Tory. She hadn't noticed him yet, so he studied her face. He'd dated many women, lived with several and briefly tried marriage over the years. He often wondered what, if any, similarities they all shared. The only commonality he'd been able to put his finger on was an awareness and appreciation that each of them had for life. Generally, this extended to everything they did. Passion and intensity were other words that came to mind. All the women he'd ever been attracted to loved food, sex, laughter and challenges. They played active roles in their lives, eschewing passive voyeurism like Instagram and Facebook, preferring instead to do things. He sensed such a force in Tory, and he wanted to learn more about her. She was also damned cute.

After a while she felt his gaze and turned towards him and smiled back somewhat shyly in recognition. At the cigarette/raffle break he went over and reintroduced himself.

"It's nice to see you again Tory, and here of all places. I'm pretty good at spotting AA people and when we met earlier today, I wouldn't have guessed."

"Same here, considering I met you sitting on a bar stool. Generally, the only alcoholics I meet in bars are still drinking, although on second thought you do seem to have a telling look of desperation about you."

Ryan thought she was serious for a second and found himself at a loss for words. She sensed his discomfort, "Hey, I'm only kidding! Don't worry, you look fine." She reached out and touched his shoulder reassuringly.

"Actually, I was just being nice. When I first saw you, I said to myself, well here comes another skid row, welfare mom if I've ever seen one. They come into The Black Watch all the time." Before even half the words out of his mouth, Tory's expression changed as something inside her shut down.

'Oh shit,' Ryan thought. 'Here I am trying to be funny and make an impression and I've totally screwed things up.'

Tory was still polite and mumbled a few more pleasantries before sitting again, but he guessed that what he'd said in jest had somehow been very hurtful. Another speaker stepped up to the podium, and he knew he could do nothing to repair things that evening and decided he would try to look her up the following day to apologize. He left after the next speaker and headed back to Parthenia.

Even though it was late October the ocean still retained some of its summer heat and as he drew closer to the water the visibility dropped. A thick layer of ground fog hung over the waterfront as the warmer water interacted with the chilly autumn air. After parking in front of their shed Ryan untied Clifton from the back of the truck and the two of them walked down to the end of the pier to sit. Between his breakup with Michelle, the incidents with the yacht owner and putting his foot in his mouth with Tory at the AA meeting, he felt like he needed a few minutes at the water's edge. Reaching the end of the pier Ryan took his normal seat on the bench and sat there in the night mist absorbing the sounds and smells that surrounded him. The flush of a school of minnows as they broke the surface of the water under the pier; the little

21

cracking sounds that the barnacles on the pilings made as the tide went out; and the gentle lapping sounds that the dinghies on the float below made as they kissed the small waves moving beneath them. The air, although cool, was heavy and musty with the smell of salt and the wet, fallen leaves that had started to rot on the ground. Slowly, the day's tensions left him.

"Soon enough," he thought to himself. "I'll be back out on the ocean and away from people and all the problems that come with them."

In the distance the White Lady appeared as a surreal glow through the fog and as he walked back up to the shed he could hear the muffled sound of her diesel generators. He thought for a moment he might have heard a yell or muffled scream above the murmur of the engines but wasn't certain. "It's none of my business," he thought, "I have enough problems of my own and don't need to add to the list."

***

White Lady weighed anchor a half-hour later and started steaming south. Below, Edward stood in front of one of the full-length mirrors in his brightly lit stateroom and admired his oiled image.

"You are looking good Edward," he said out loud and ran his hands over his slick body, stopping to fondle and pull at his large cock, still wet and distended after the evening's activities. "Yes, you are quite something."

He continued to preen and strut in front of the mirror for a few more moments before deciding that it was time for another generous line of nose candy. He walked back to the bed in a narcotic fog and looked down at the woman that was laying still, leaking, onto his sheets. "What a stupid, stupid cunt," he thought.

"Well at least she makes a good table." He leaned over her naked and blistered stomach and snorted a line of coke off her now quiet chest. The burn felt good as he jacked the line into the back of his nose, and he toyed with the idea of having sex with her again. "She'd always been a dead fuck anyway," he thought to himself.

"How about it Charlene," he said as he poked her, "one for the road?" He laughed at his little joke then got up off the bed and wandered

22

aimlessly around the room straightening books, lining things up on the bedside table and muttering to himself, "Must clean up this mess, everything, so untidy." He moved around the room not really cleaning up anything but rather obsessively rearranging things. After a few minutes Charlene's burnt and beaten body intruded back into his consciousness and he realized that she was the reason why his sense of order was disturbed. In a sudden rage he grabbed the sheet she was laying on and ripped it off the bed, her body tumbling onto the floor on the other side of the bed.

"Fucking bitch!" he yelled. He threw on a robe and wrenched open the door. "Manuel, get your sorry ass in here!"

Manuel had been awake since retiring an hour earlier, unable to sleep for the sounds that were coming from the adjoining cabin. He cringed at the sound of Edward's voice wondering what the sick bastard wanted. From the moment they'd left the restaurant he knew there would be trouble because of all the drugs and alcohol Edward had consumed. The scene with the waitress and Edward's subsequent dressing down by Mr. Slade on the way back to the boat had not helped matters. Manuel hurried out of bed and into a pair of jeans before sticking his head out of the door.

"Si, I'm coming!" If it weren't for his generous salary, he would have been gone months ago. To his way of thinking Edward was a vicious sadist and unstable as all hell. Also, his drug consumption of late had been off the rails. He had seen Charlene with bruises from their "lovemaking" before but it in no way prepared for what he saw lying on the floor next to the bed when he walked into Edward's cabin. He knew right away that she was likely dead from the volume of blood on the sheet that covered her and the silence that pervaded the room, but he turned her over anyway. She was bound with her hands behind her back and gagged. Her jaw was broken and several of her teeth were broken or missing. What really got to Manuel, however, were the horrible burns all over her body. In some areas the skin was entirely blackened and burned away, in others, fat red blisters evidenced the incredible violence that had been inflicted on the poor girl. Manuel saw the small propane

23

torch that Edward used to light his crack pipe lying on the edge of the bed and knew that this must have been what he had used.

"What the fuck man, what'd you do to her? She was just a sweet, simple hooker. What could she have done to deserve this?" Manuel was no stranger to violence and had hurt people himself doing enforcement work, but this went beyond, into a world that even Manuel could not understand.

Edward was speechless for a moment and then went into a rage and started slapping the back of Manuel's head like an abusive parent might strike his child. It was not as much painful as humiliating, and Manuel thought of the waitress in the restaurant. "Don't you ever speak to me like that again you wet-back fuck! You're nothing without me and you'll speak respectfully to me. Do. You. Understand?" He slapped Manuel's head three more times to emphasize each of his last three words.

Hating himself for taking the abuse, yet unwilling to challenge him further, he replied meekly, "Si, Senor Edward, I understand."

"Now, get rid of this piece of shit, she's messing up my rug!" Edward turned and walked into the adjoining toilet.

Manuel touched Charlene's face tenderly and shook his head thinking of some conversations they'd shared. No one deserved this. He continued to kneel at her side for a moment holding his emotions in check and then gently gathered her up in the sheet and carried her out onto the deck and then to the stern. He held her in his arms until they tired and then he let her slide into the waiting sea. She disappeared in the churning wake. 'These are not the things that my father brought me up to do,' he thought with self-disgust.

Paulo stepped out from the shadows as Manuel turned to head back to his stateroom. Manuel and he were not close. Paulo was sneaky and always seemed to be in the shadows scurrying from place to place like the rodent he resembled. He had a pockmarked face, was built like an anorexic, and had two front teeth that were askew and angled forward. He never bathed and Manuel was embarrassed when he had to go anywhere in public with him.

"What do you want Paulo?"

"I could not sleep for the noises that were coming from Senor Edward's cabin. She sounded very excited, no?"

Manuel couldn't believe what he was hearing. Paulo had obviously been turned on by the torture. For a moment he had this horrible dark vision of Paulo masturbating in his cabin to the sounds of Charlene being tortured.

"I am surprised that you did not have a little piece yourself before throwing her over," Paulo added.

Manuel's impotence and loathing boiled to the surface and he grabbed Paulo by his skinny, acne covered neck. "You are the lowest form of life I can imagine." He said as he continued to tighten his grasp around Paolo's throat. "If I ever hear the word 'Charlene' come from your rancid little mouth again, I'll break your neck and then stomp on you until every bone in your worthless little body is broken."

He was so focused in his hatred for Paulo that he momentarily forgot the stiletto blade that was never more than a few inches from Paulo's hand. Paulo chose that moment to bring the knife up between them with just enough pressure that the tip of the blade pierced Manuel's shirt and barely punctured the skin about an inch below his sternum. It was not Paulo's intention to kill him, but the placement and pressure were adequate to convey his ability to do so if he chose. Manuel eased his grip in response.

"I hear you Manuel. Now is not the time, but I would be very careful to sleep with one eye open in the future. Comprende?"

Manuel held his position for a moment longer against the pressure of the blade. "Better than you know Paulo. I meant what I said about the girl, remember that." He turned and walked back to his cabin.

Chapter 2

Ryan woke up depressed, thinking about how he'd screwed up the night before, rolled over and went back to sleep till 7:30. He was re-awakened by Clifton's excited moaning on the ground below the boat. A few seconds later someone knocked on the outside of the hull. Ryan reluctantly swung his legs over the side of the bunk, threw on a pair of jeans, climbed up on deck and started to look over the side.

"What do want?" he started in a gruff, annoyed voice. He looked down from the deck. It was Tory and she was smiling. Ryan's mood did a complete 180.

"Well hi! What a nice surprise."

"Whatcha doing?"

"I guess I was waiting for you guys to get here so we could all go out for breakfast. What kept you?"

Tory beamed back at him.

"Give me a sec. I'll be right down." Everything was suddenly right. He felt like a teenager who had just been acknowledged by the prettiest girl in class and quickly brushed his hair and teeth and threw on a clean T-shirt. He was on his way down the ladder three minutes later.

Tory was sitting on one of the staging planks that surrounded the boat and watched as he descended. He turned to her at the bottom and was again stricken by the positive energy that seemed to surround her.

"Tory, before I say anything else, I owe you an apology," Ryan began.

"No, it's the other way around. I owe you an apology. When you saw me at the meeting last night, I was feeling a little lost and shaky and not terribly sure of myself. I was probably way too sensitive. You were just giving back what you got in jest and I took what you said all wrong. It was my fault," she replied.

"No, it definitely wasn't your fault. It was mine, really. Sometimes I engage my mouth before thinking. I'm really sorry and hope you'll forgive me. I get flustered around beautiful women and say really stupid things sometimes."

Tory blushed shyly for a moment at his compliment. "Were you serious about breakfast? We're actually starved."

"Absolutely, I know a great place about five minutes from here."

"We'd like that, thanks."

Ryan smiled. "Your car or mine?"

"It will have to be yours because we walked. C'mon kids, we're going out for breakfast."

"Is Clifton coming?" Jan asked.

"Yes, he's coming," Ryan replied as he opened the tailgate of the truck so Clifton could jump in.

"Can I ride in the back with him?" Jan asked.

Ryan turned to Tory leaving the question hanging in the air. "It's fine with me. It's only a short ride."

Tory thought about it for a second. "I guess so. Just make sure you stay sitting Jan and don't move around."

"Can I too, Mom?" Willy asked.

"No sweetie, you ride up front with us. Besides, you like big trucks and maybe Ryan will let you steer."

"Let him steer? How old is he, about five?"

"He's a very attentive driver for his age. You'll be surprised. Trust me,"

Ryan didn't want to say or do anything that might upset the rapport that was developing between them. "I assume the little nipper will sit on my lap or shall I see if I can't dig up a few phone books?"

"No, he'll sit on your lap and steer. You handle the gas and the brakes and tell him where you want him to go. He can't reach the pedals yet."

Ryan settled Jan and Clifton in the back and then after adjusting his seat back a bit, took Willy on his lap. "Well, here we go. Let's just hope we don't run into any cops on the way."

Ryan put the truck in gear and gave it a little gas. Tory was smiling like a Cheshire Cat at Ryan's discomfort. He had Willy steer into the parking lot and then had him do a few circles to get a feel for his capabilities and to also give him a little time to get used to the truck. After the quick refresher they slowly made their way out of the dirt lot and out onto the main road leading back into town. Ryan had to admit, the kid was good, and he was amused as the young child did his determined best to steer a straight course. He liked children but had never felt squared away or responsible enough to have any of his own. When he did spend time with kids, he found he enjoyed their company, especially when they were teachable and anxious to learn something he had to offer. Willy was incredibly focused as he maintained a relatively straight course down the road.

"Willy, you're a pretty darn good driver," Ryan finally admitted.

"Told you," Tory replied.

They reached the Silver Spoon several minutes later and tumbled out leaving Clifton tied in the back. The Silver Spoon was busy with a weekend crowd and as soon as they were seated a waitress brought over some crayons for Willy to draw on his placemat with. Jan also joined in after a few minutes. Tory and Ryan turned to each other and although both were a little nervous at first, they were soon talking as easily as old friends might and quickly became oblivious to everything going on around them. When Jan or Willy would ask a question or for something to be passed, Tory responded in an almost autonomic fashion, her eyes and attention seldom wandering from Ryan. He was equally rapt, and 45 minutes passed quickly as they ate and talked.

"Mom, don't forget about the aquarium," Jan reminded Tory.

Tory looked at her watch. "Shoot, I totally forgot!" She turned to Ryan. "I'm sorry, it totally slipped my mind, but I promised them weeks ago that we would go to The New England Aquarium up in Boston today and we were supposed to meet my friends 10 minutes ago. Would you mind running us back to their house? They wanted to leave by 9:30."

Ryan was disappointed that their time would be cut short, but said, "No, I'd be happy to." After haggling with Tory over the bill, she finally allowed him to pay with the understanding that there would be a second meal soon and that she would pay for that one.

Tory's friend Stephanie already had her coat on and walked out of the house to greet them as they drove up the driveway. Ryan and Stephanie had never been formally introduced, but they recognized each other from the post office and passing on the street and talked for a while about local happenings while Tory got the kids ready to go. A few minutes later they emerged from the house with Stephanie's husband Bill and introductions were made again.

Stephanie turned to Tory. "Are you sure you don't want to come?"

"No, I really want a little time to myself and I want to get unpacked and do some of our laundry. I've already been to the Aquarium anyway. You guys go and have a good time."

Tory turned to Ryan with a smile as Bill, Stephanie, and the two children disappeared down the driveway. "What are you doing today?"

Ryan was excited about the turn of events and the possibility of spending more time with her. "I do have a lot of work to do on the boat, but I guess I could take a few hours off to do something with you if you wanted?"

"What if I helped you? I don't know a lot about boats, but I'm sure there's something I could do, and we could talk more as we work."

Despite his excitement, Ryan knew he was about to complicate his life and chastised himself for all of three or four seconds before saying, "yes" and taking her up on her offer. Tory went back into the house to change into work clothes. Ryan shook his head at his lack of resolve and ticked off the reasons in his mind why it was a bad idea to even think about starting anything with this new woman. Not only was he leaving town in several weeks, but she was in recovery and had children. He had long had a policy of not dating women in AA figuring that one lunatic was enough in any relationship. Within the confines of AA, they had an expression, "Don't shop for a new car in a junkyard."

"Please, save me from myself," he intoned to no one in particular.

As it turned out, once they got started working there was very little talk between them until lunchtime. The project Ryan set them to that morning was sanding all Parthenia's floorboards in preparation for new varnish. When they finally finished at 12:30 both were covered from head to toe in chalky white dust from the old finish. Ryan crossed the shed to get one of the compressed air hoses to blow them off.

Tory admired the result of her morning's work and marveled at how good it felt to do physical labor and to be in the company of a vibrant and attractive man. She'd spent months in the treatment center and halfway house and then had to go through weeks of court appearances and legal wrangling to regain custody of Willy and Jan. This had left her with little time to think about anything other than recovery and rebuilding the trust of her two children. Ryan was obviously interested in her and there seemed to be a chemistry between them that was both natural and exciting. It was nice to feel a part of the world again and the work they had done together that morning was both tangible and rewarding.

Ryan returned from the other side of the shed dragging one of the air hoses. "Keep your eyes closed and I'll blow you off."

He fit a straight nozzle to the hose and high-pressure air immediately started to blast out of the end of the hose. "Close your eyes," he yelled over the roar of the air.

Tory did as she was told, and Ryan started at her feet and clouds of dust filled the air as he blew the accumulated varnish dust off her. She gave herself over to the powerful blast of air that he directed up and down the fronts of her legs in a slow and determined fashion. The air seemed to become an extension of his hand and even though she was wearing coveralls over her street clothes, the sensation was strangely erotic and she felt almost naked as he worked the air-stream up and down her legs. The eroticism of the experience was not lost on Ryan and he found himself staring at her body and being much more thorough than necessary in the dust removal process. She was tight and defined at every juncture and he could easily imagine himself in bed with her. When he was done blowing her off, he redirected the stream of air onto his own clothes and after finishing, pulled the nozzle from the fitting at the end of the hose with a loud pop. They were suddenly surrounded in silence, both flushed and breathing hard despite the cool temperature.

"That was interesting," Tory remarked.

Ryan was tempted to reach out and pull her to him but restrained himself and instead dropped the hose to the floor, suddenly embarrassed by the intimacy of the experience. "I guess we should go get some lunch or something."

Tory agreed and after picking up some sandwiches at the downtown deli they returned to the boatyard and went to the end of the dock to eat in the fresh air and sunlight.

"What brings you to Sippican?" Ryan asked after a few minutes of silent eating.

She looked at him for a moment deciding how much to share. "Running, I guess. Looking for something I haven't yet found. Trying to get to know my kids again. A little peace maybe."

"Why do you have to get to know your kids again?"

Tory looked down at the ground before replying. "I had a pretty bad crack and alcohol addiction and child welfare took them from me after I got busted."

Ryan considered his reply. "I guess I understand now why my comment last night hurt like it did. How long were you separated from them?"

"About 10 months. I spent two months in a treatment facility then six more in a halfway house. The rest of the time I spent in court trying to regain custody of them."

"Didn't you have any family to take care of them?"

"Not really. Neither of my parents are alive, my ex-husband split after Willy was born, and my grandparents are pretty old. As a result, I've felt pretty worthless for the last few years. I'm a tad sensitive as a result, especially in the mom department."

"I guess I can understand that," Ryan agreed. "So how did you end up here in Sippican?"

"It's a long story, but the three of us have mostly lived in and around cities and I don't want Jan and Willy to grow up in that environment. We're basically on the road looking for a better lifestyle, school system, place to be. You know, something more. I figured this was a nice, small New England town and I already had friends here, so why not check it out?" her voice trailed off momentarily. "What's your story?" Tory asked, hoping to deflect some of the attention away from herself.

"Well, I'm 37 years old and still don't have a clue as to what I want to be when I grow up. I've been sober longer than you but basically, I want to try something totally different. Last year I got into a dispute with the IRS and ended up with a tax obligation that forced me to sell my house and I've basically decided, screw it. I'm fed up with all of it; taxes, crime, business, materialism, debt, television ads, big government, the works. I've finally mustered up enough courage to take off on my boat, something I've wanted to do for years. I have a little cash stashed away from the sale of my house and some marketable trade skills. I finally figured out that the only way you can ever do something new and different is to just do it."

Ryan continued a few seconds later. "You know, a lot of people say they're going to do what I'm doing, but they always qualify it with, "when I have enough money, or when the kids are settled in college, or when my parents die." It's always qualified with 'when'. I don't think there's ever a perfect time to do anything. You just get older and one day you wake up and you realize you're too old to do most of the things you'd planned. I know I'm an escapist at heart, but if that's really me why not just be me instead of pretending year after year that I'm someone else. I don't know how long it will last but I'm doing it and leaving on Parthenia in three weeks' time for the Caribbean."

They finished their sandwiches in silence and were sipping the last of their sodas when Tory spoke again.

"Ryan, I know this is going to sound ridiculously impulsive and a little crazy to you, but I learned a long time ago that if you never ask, nothing happens. I also know we hardly know each other, but would you consider the possibility of taking the three of us with you?"

Ryan was momentarily speechless. Obviously, she was crazy. When he did finally speak, he surprised them both.

"I might. I was thinking of bringing along one or two crew for the passage south anyway." He slapped himself on both sides of his face and smiling said, "Wait a minute, did I just say what I think I did?"

Tory didn't say anything and simply sat looking into his face earnestly until he spoke again.

"You're serious, aren't you?"

Tory nodded.

"I'll consider it. I've taken all kinds of crew on lots of trips and it would be nice to have some company on the way south. I guess my main hesitation is I don't really know what my responsibility would be to the three of you. I'm looking to reduce my commitments, not add to them. Also, I hardly know you."

"Ryan, I'm not asking you to marry me. I'm just talking about a ride south." she countered defensively.

"But where will you go once we get South? What will you do for money and work? What about schooling for the kids? I don't want to just give you a ride down there and drop you off in the middle of nowhere with no plan."

"That's so male. It's OK for you to up and leave with no plan, but not for a woman? I know it sounds impulsive, but think about it, I've been looking for a better life and a fresh start for me and the kids. We have a second chance now and I believe that whatever we choose to do with our lives from this moment on will be OK if I just stay sober and we stay together as a family. I love those two more than my own life. If it was just me, I think I would have chosen to die a year ago in a crack house. My self-loathing was bottomless, and I was willing to do anything, and I mean anything for a rock of crack. I couldn't have gotten any lower as a woman," Tory paused for a second. "I don't have to do that anymore. I want to suck everything I can from this second chance."

"But what about Willy and Jan? The schools down there can't offer half of what's available here."

"Oh Ryan, be real. What half are you worried they'll miss? The bullying, hard drugs in elementary school or maybe all the porn and violence they'll get exposed to by the age of 14? I want my kids to become a part of the solution rather than being a part of the problem. I want them to grow up with healthy values, to be self-sufficient, respectful of other people and to have a sense of self-worth. None of those things are taught in schools anymore. As for their traditional schooling; before I was a crack addict, I was a grammar school teacher, so I know I can teach them the basics on my own. When they get to be college age, they can make their own decisions about where they want to go and who they want to be."

"What about money?" he asked.

"That's covered. It's not a lot but I stayed close to my grandfather even through the worst of it and he set up a trust fund that provides me with a monthly check that's enough to cover our basic needs. I won't have access to any of the principal for another 10 years because he's afraid that I might go back to using drugs again, but it's enough to get by."

Ryan just sat looking at her, taking her in for a few more moments. "Let me think about it for a few days. In the meantime, we have work to do." He smiled at her and they both got up and headed back up the dock to put on the first of many coats of varnish that would go on the floorboards they'd sanded earlier. As they walked Ryan had the feeling he'd forgotten something and turned back and looked out over the harbor. The White Lady was gone. He'd been so preoccupied with Tory and all that had transpired since awakening that morning that he'd totally forgotten about the confrontation with the man off the boat the night before.

Rip Converse

Chapter 3

Over the next couple of weeks, fall firmly established itself over the New England coast. The last of the leaves colored and fell lazily to ground, the temperature began its sly descent and chainsaws growled angrily in backwoods lots. Ryan loved this time of year for the local harvests of apples, cranberries and pumpkins, but also knew that these were only sacraments passed out by nature to prepare everyone for another damp, dismal, New England winter.

After their initial conversation as to whether Tory and her children might join him on the trip south, they had spoken little more about it. They had, instead, settled quite naturally into a daily routine that left little doubt as to how many would be crewing Parthenia to the tropics. Each morning Tory dropped Jan off at school and Willy at day-care, then drove to the boatyard to spend the day working with Ryan; sanding, painting, measuring, running errands and doing whatever else needed doing to ready Parthenia for the trip south. They frequently talked and joked with each other about sex and getting involved, but their relationship remained platonic. Both were aware that something special might be growing between them and were content to simply let it grow while basking in the increasing awareness and sensitivity each was developing for the other rather than rushing headlong into a relationship. It was a first for both. Except for an occasional pizza and AA meeting together, they generally spent their evenings alone. Ryan tinkered with electronics aboard Parthenia and Tory stayed home with the children helping with homework and generally trying to make up for all the time they had spent apart. Parthenia was finally scheduled for launching on November 13, in two days' time, and the only remaining project was to roll on several fresh coats of bottom paint hours before the launch. After she was in the water they would fill her storage lockers with the mountains of canned and dry-goods they'd be taking South.

Piracy by drug runners was an increasing concern to mariners frequenting certain areas of the Bahamas and Caribbean, particularly in the areas of the Mona and Windward Passages. Ryan had sailed many times down in the islands with no bad experiences. However, on this trip he decided it would not be a bad idea to have some form of protection on board. Just the year before, two very close friends of his had disappeared while cruising in the Caribbean and were assumed lost at sea until the boat finally turned up three weeks later in the Florida Keys half sunk. After the smugglers were done with it, they opened all the seacocks, then abandoned it to sink to the bottom. The vessel came to rest on a shallow shelf with the masthead protruding just above the surface. A passing vessel reported the boat and, after a search by Coast Guard divers, the bodies of his two friends were found bound and gagged in the forward stateroom. Autopsies revealed that both had died from gunshot wounds. With the added responsibility of Tory and the children, Ryan decided to bring a handgun and a shotgun with them.

He didn't want to scare Tory or make too big a deal out of it and decided to build a small storage compartment in the starboard sail locker, which he did over the course of two evenings without her knowledge. The challenge was to make it secretive in construction so that nothing would be found during routine customs inspections. Perhaps more importantly he made it so that the children wouldn't inadvertently stumble across it while playing. The solution he'd come up with was a fiberglass, hinged box that he mounted on the inside of the sail locker. It looked like an electrical junction box to the casual observer. For added realism he ran several of the existing antenna wires through both sides of the box so that anyone looking over the boat would in fact assume that the purpose of the box was the protection of these cables. It looked like a permanent enclosure, but by reaching under and pulling out a pin that ran through a long piano type hinge, the entire box simply fell away and allowed access to the guns which snapped into place in rubber coated brackets. He hoped they'd never need them but felt it better to be safe than sorry.

Launch day finally arrived, and Tory kept both children home so they could participate in the long-awaited event.

"Tory, did you tie off all those wooden plugs near each through-hull fitting like I asked?"

"Yes Ryan."

"Did you find that box of clevis pins and cotter pins?"

"Yes Ryan."

"Did you get out the two big screwdrivers and the vice grips?"

"Yes Ryan! Would you try and relax a little! Everything's ready." And then added a deferential, "Sir!"

"Tory, please don't bust my chops right now, I want to be ready when the truck gets here. These guys are on a tight schedule at this time of year and if we aren't ready exactly at high tide we will have to wait until tomorrow to put her in the water."

"I know Ryan, it's just that we've checked and double checked everything and I'm sure we're ready. It'll be alright."

Tory was in fact as nervous as Ryan and had a vested interest in Parthenia by virtue of the long weeks of labor she'd put in helping to get her ready for launch. Jan and Willy weren't helping the situation as they ran circles around the base of the boat playing with Clifton. Tory tried yelling at them and Ryan had sent Clifton to his bed with stern warnings and threats of severe bodily injury several times, but they all sensed the excitement and only stayed quiet for a few moments at a time before resuming their chasing games.

The long-bed hydraulic truck that would transport Parthenia finally pulled into the yard at about 9:20 a.m. With it came a companion crane truck that would transport the mast and spars separately the short distance to the launch site. The long-bed hydraulic truck never ceased to amaze Ryan even though he'd probably launched and hauled Parthenia 25 times in the previous 10 years. The skill of the drivers to maneuver the massive trailers into small areas to pick up and unload vessels was legendary. For all their skill however, Ryan was always nervous when they transported Parthenia because she was wood and subsequently more vulnerable out of the water than a fiberglass boat.

A small crowd consisting of yard workers and other boat owners had gathered to watch the operation. As the trailer pulled Parthenia out into the light there was a small smattering of applause. Ryan and Tory looked on with pride at the result of their labors. At this moment in time, Parthenia looked as good as she had 30 years before when she was first launched. Every surface was freshly coated with paint or mirror-like varnish and the winches and fittings were polished and sparkling to a high shine. Even though nature would begin to reverse this process with salt, sun and wind the moment she was launched, on this morning she was stunning and the envy of all.

Ryan rode on the deck of Parthenia to help push aside branches and hold up low overhanging wires as they headed down the small overgrown country road that led to the launching site. Tory followed behind in Ryan's pickup with Clifton and the children. Willy was full of questions. The fact that they were actually leaving had finally fallen within his six-year-old frame of reality. It was happening *now*, not in some future time frame like next month or next week. "Mom, where will I sleep? Will it tip over if we get in a storm? Will whales eat us? What happens if I fall overboard?"

Tory did her best to answer his questions. She was as excited as he was and felt as though they were about to embark on a great adventure.

When they got to the public wharf and landing, there was another crowd of people, mostly retirees who liked to sit on the benches along the wharf sipping coffee and watching the fishing boats come and go. It was a busy time of year with winter haul-outs going on and there was much for them to discuss and argue over. There was one boat ahead of Parthenia being hauled onto another trailer in the slip they'd be going down which gave Tory a chance to park Ryan's truck and herd the children over to the boat. Ryan lowered down a stepladder from Parthenia's deck for them to climb up so that they could all be together as Parthenia was backed down the slipway and into the water. Just as he got the last of them seated in the cockpit, the other trailer pulled out and Tommy, the driver of their truck, shouted up to see if they were ready and ran through his pre-launch check list like he did with all boat owners.

"You all set up there Ryan?"

"I think so."

"Through-hulls for the engine open? Lines ready? Fenders out?"

"Yup, yup, yup. Let's run her in and see if she floats." Ryan did not want to miss the tide and it would be close. Parthenia drew almost 7 feet of water and at dead high tide it was only about 7'4" in the slip they were in. It had already peaked and started down.

On Ryan's say so, Tommy disengaged the trailer from the tractor and started to let it roll backwards down the slip into the water, controlling the trailer's speed by regulating the hydraulic drum that fed out cable from the rear of the tractor. This cable was attached to the trailer. When the trailer had rolled as far back as it could into the water, Ryan started the new diesel then ran below to check for leaks. The hydraulic arms that supported Parthenia were still engaged and gripping her fore and aft on either side. Ryan pulled up several floorboards and checked the major through-hull fittings looking for leaks. With the exception of a steady drip that was coming in around the stuffing box, Parthenia was ready. He expected the boat would have minor leaks for several days as the wood swelled up but that was normal for a wooden boat that had been out of the water for several months.

"OK Tommy, let her go!" Ryan yelled.

Tommy maneuvered the hydraulic arms away from their support positions, and Parthenia was left floating on her own. Ryan slipped the motor into reverse and they inched off the trailer until they were clear of the trailer then slowly backed their way out of the slipway and out into open water. Then he positioned fenders along the port side of the boat and tied off to the outer pier. The crane truck then drove down the pier until it was abreast of them and lifted the mast and rigging into the air so that it could be lowered through the hole in Parthenia's deck and onto the mast step on top of the keel in the main salon below. With Tory and Tommy's help he was able to guide it safely through the deck hole and seat it securely on the mast step. The crane truck stayed in place for several minutes while Ryan pounded in the blocks of wood that held the mast securely in the center of the hole where it passed through the deck and then he loosely fastened the fore and aft stays. Tommy helped by connecting the inner shrouds on either side. The crane then disconnected from the mast and drove off down the pier towards their next client.

Ryan came up on deck with his checkbook. "What do I owe you Tommy?"

"Three hundred will do it. You guys have a safe trip and don't stay away too long."

"Thanks Tom. You take care of yourself too."

They all waved as he walked off the pier and for the first time in months Ryan felt like it was all really going to happen. It hadn't been easy for him moving out of his house and into the confines of a boat full time, but now that their departure was imminent the possibilities represented in Parthenia's gentle motion in the water seemed limitless and the decision felt completely right. He looked over at Tory and smiled.

"Feels good, doesn't it?" Ryan really was excited, and he could see that excitement mirrored in Tory's eyes. He gave her a long hug.

"Thanks for your help, the boat has never looked better and allot of it is your work. You did well."

Tory blushed at the compliment. "You know each day we got closer to leaving I knew this was a good decision for me and for Willy and Jan. This is a big deal to us too."

Willy suddenly ran by them on deck and Ryan yelled out, "Whoa! Sport, wait." Willy stopped.

"Until you learn how to swim, I'm afraid you're going to have to wear a life preserver on deck, at all times; even when we're tied up at the dock. Understand?" Ryan was looking back and forth between Tory and Willy as he laid down the rule. He wanted Tory's support on this.

Willy looked up at Tory. "Do I have to Mom?"

"Absolutely. When we are on this boat, Ryan is captain and his rules are inviolate." She rolled her eyes as she said this. To give absolute power to anyone went against her grain, but she did happen to agree with this particular rule.

"Mom, what does in-violate mean?"

Tory thought for a moment and then said with a smile, "It means that a rule absolutely, positively cannot be broken unless it is done by the second in command, which happens to be me. Any other questions?"

"No, I guess not. But how come Jan doesn't have to wear one?"

"Because she's a good swimmer. You'll learn soon enough. Here let me help you on with yours." She reached into the portside cockpit locker, pulled out a child size life preserver, and helped him into it before he ran off.

"No. 2, I couldn't help but notice that you seem to have a rather loose interpretation of the word inviolate. I note that you've exempted yourself?"

Tory smiled at him. "Through necessity due to your well known and deserved reputation for strange and perverse proclivities of a sexual nature."

Ryan feigned outrage. "That's pretty harsh. Do you think you know me well enough to make such a judgement?"

"Oh, I think I've got your number sailor." Tory reached out and tickled him under the arm."

Ryan tickled her back using both hands. Tory tried to pull away. "You bastard!"

"Mum, I heard that, 75 cents," Willy shouted from below. Tory and Ryan burst out laughing.

They spent the rest of the morning rigging Parthenia, getting all the stay and shroud tensions adjusted so that the mast would stand straight and secure in the boat with just a slight rake backwards. Then, after a quick run back to the boatyard for the sails, they hanked the mainsail onto the boom and stowed the rest of the sails in the foc'sle and the aft sail locker.

By the time they were finished it was almost two and the kids were hungry and bored. Ryan talked it over with Tory and they decided to take a shakedown sail the following morning and do the food shopping immediately afterward. Ryan had warned her that none of them would feel like cooking or eating much the first few days out at sea due to possible seasickness and it was Tory's plan to make and freeze several casseroles that afternoon and evening.

Ryan had a multitude of small projects he hoped to accomplish before they sailed and after running everyone back to Bill and Stephanie's, he returned to the boatyard to get the Zodiac outboard, inflatable life raft, and Gerry jugs for spare fuel. The inflatable Zodiac was already deflated and in its bag. Ryan stowed it below, behind the navigator's berth and then screwed the Yamaha outboard tightly to a transom board he'd rigged off the stern pulpit.

The life raft was a bigger problem and required the assistance of several pier watchers to get the heavy canister on board and in place on the cabin roof forward of the main hatch. This particular raft held six adults in relative comfort when inflated, and when not, it resided in a hard-plastic case that was lashed securely to the cabin top.

Ryan had tremendous faith in the construction of Parthenia and her ability to withstand the fiercest of storms. A secondary concern of his was the increasing volume of debris drifting in the world's oceans and the threat it represented to a wooden hulled boat. Chief among these are metal containers that have been swept off cargo ships in storms. If Parthenia were to hit one of these it could easily stove in her planks and take her to the bottom. The life raft gave them a second chance if the worst were ever to happen.

As Ryan finished securing the life raft canister on the cabin roof a voice called down to him from above on the dock. "Got room for another crew?"

Clifton gave out one pathetic woof and then stood up with his tail wagging. Ryan looked up. "Hey Chris, it's good to see you! How are you, a little early for you to be home from the office isn't it?"

Chris climbed down the ladder to the deck and shook Ryan's hand and then, thinking better of it, gave him a quick, awkward hug.

"Well I wasn't sure whether you were leaving tomorrow morning or the day after and I wanted to be sure to come by and give you a little shit for actually doing what all of us want to do."

Chris and Ryan had sailed and raced together many times over the years and their relationship went back as far as high school. Growing up together they'd shared many of the same interests, friends and even girlfriends, although in recent years they'd been spending less and less time together. To Ryan's way of thinking, Chris had more responsibilities than God. He had four kids, multiple homes, several successful businesses and a debt load that would frighten a congressman.

"You are such a dog. Still single, taking off on your boat for the islands with a beautiful new girlfriend and just saying "fuck it" to everything else. I wish I had your balls."

Ryan looked into his eyes and replied, "Don't kid yourself. Balls don't have anything to do with it. I just can't take it anymore. I'm bailing out buddy. Hey, I've got some coffee brewing below. Want a cup?"

"No, I'm fine." There was an uncomfortable silence for several seconds and Ryan nervously tried to fill it.

"Nothing seems to feel right anymore around here for me. I've been feeling like I'm reading lines in a play I don't really want to act in anymore," Ryan realized what he was saying probably sounded a bit heavy to Chris and didn't want to scare him off right away so went to safer ground.

"What about you? How are Heather and the kids?"

Happy to fill the silence Chris went on for several minutes about his oldest daughter who had just gotten into B.U., his youngest who was just starting to date, his wife's newest store and wrapped it up sharing his woes about his new ski condominium and the outrageousness of his most recent service bill on his Mercedes.

Ryan did his best to congratulate and commiserate with him on the various topics he brought up but had difficulty identifying and expressing any convincing sincerity. Like the past few times they had spoken, Ryan sensed the flatness in their interaction. Chris did too and after an uncomfortable pause asked, "But Ryan, what about a couple of years from now? I mean, I'm not suggesting that you need three cars and two houses and five million bucks in the bank to be happy, but don't you want the freedom to just kick back later in life?"

"Kick back? What does that mean, shuffling back and forth between the yacht club and golf club for the rest of my life? I spent years chasing money and the insulation it buys from the rest of the world and I want to do more, not less. I'm not saying I want to suffer or be penniless in my old age, but I do want to experience and feel, and I'm hoping to find some of that on this trip. And you know what? When I was selling my house and all the other crap I'd accumulated over the last 37 years, I didn't feel like I was losing anything. I just felt lighter and lighter with every trip to the dump, like I could finally breathe again."

Chris kept nodding and looking him in the eyes as he spoke, but Ryan could see there was no real understanding. Chris had that slightly vacant look people get when they feel no connection to what's being said. They hear the words but can't relate them to their own lives.

"Well, I'm not sure I understand exactly what it is that you think you're missing or what you hope to find, but whatever it is, I really hope you find it buddy."

Ryan knew his words were heartfelt. But he also knew with a certain sadness and finality that the gulf that had been growing between them in recent years was finally larger than the bridge of their shared youth and experiences and that this conversation would probably be their last for a long time.

"Chris, as outrageous as all this may seem to you, I want you to know that I appreciate your friendship and support."

They hugged again and Chris climbed the ladder back onto the dock. He turned at the top. "Want to come up to The Black Watch for a quick pop with me, you know, for old times' sake?"

Ryan knew Chris would more than likely have three or four "pops" and just smiled and said, "No, I don't think so. I've got a lot to do here on the boat tonight and you know me anyway, one is too many and a thousand's not enough."

"Still not drinking huh?"

"I don't have to anymore."

Chris shook his head and with one last look backwards, waved and strolled down the pier to The Black Watch.

Ryan indulged in a little self-pity for a few moments that he wasn't joining Chris for a drink and thought of all the other old friends that had slowly faded from his life since he'd gotten sober. He missed them at times, but it really wasn't his abstinence or their unavailability that made him sad but more the fact that many of them now bored him. A few were full blown alcoholics as he'd been, with all the attendant drama and marital problems that go along with heavy drinking. The majority, however, lived stuck, in a horrible limbo world, able to manage their increasing dependence, but settling for second best in everything they did in the process. It was as if they were sound asleep as their country-club lives passed before them. Ryan sat down at his nav station to program latitude and longitude waypoints into the GPS, grateful for the possibility in his own life.

Tory returned at 8 p.m. with a plate of food knowing that Ryan had probably not eaten. The temperature had fallen to the mid-forties and Ryan had the hatches closed and the propane stove on for warmth. She stuck her head through the companionway hatch.

"God, it's cold out here. Nice and toasty in here though. How's it going?"

Ryan was hunched over the navigation table and hadn't heard her set foot on board as he was running the engine and charging the batteries trying to get the refrigerator/freezer down to temperature.

"Hey beautiful, it's going good." Ryan got up off his seat and took the aluminum-covered plate she held out to him as she came down the ladder.

"What did you bring me?"

"Lasagna and garlic bread."

"Sounds perfect for a cold fall evening. That reminds me, I've been so busy screwing around with the GPS I forgot to feed the little pup."

"I'll do it while you eat."

Tory adored Clifton and scratched lovingly behind his ears. As Ryan started to eat his meal Tory fished around for a can of dog food out of one of the storage lockers and mixed it with dry food and placed the bowl up in the cockpit with Clifton so she and Ryan could eat and talk in peace without feeling guilty.

"How're the kids?" Ryan asked.

"I put Willy to bed before coming down here and Jan is still up with Bill and Stephanie going through an atlas trying to figure the distances between here and Bermuda, and Bermuda and the Caribbean. They're both so excited. I think Jan's packed and repacked her duffel bag three times already today." Tory sat down beside Ryan on the navigator's berth and watched him eat.

"So, tell me a little more what it will be like offshore."

Ryan thought for a few moments between bites, "Well, you know what they say about yachting?"

"No, what do *they* say about yachting?"

"That it's the most expensive way to travel third class. It gets pretty small in here," Ryan gestured around the cabin.

"The four of us will be cramped together in this one small floating room, heeled over at an awkward angle for days at a time. Bathing is rare, cooking is difficult, and you'll probably never be as tired as you'll get offshore, especially if we run into bad weather. Also, you'll spend more time with yourself and your thoughts than you ever have before."

"Sounds ... really fun," Tory replied without much conviction.

"Actually, I've tried many times to tell people what it's like and I never seem to do a very good job. It means different things to different people and you'll either love it or hate it. For me, a great deal of it revolves around the satisfaction I get from being able to adapt to whatever comes up. Keeping any boat afloat at sea involves your ability to keep a lot of different forces in balance which means that you have to be aware of what's going on around you, and second, to be ready to respond appropriately to constantly changing conditions. It requires presence and mindfulness and you know, it's funny, I guess that's where the escape comes in for me because you don't have time to think about any of your other life problems when 100 percent of your focus is on keeping the boat afloat and moving in the direction you want to go. I love it." Ryan liked talking about the subject and continued.

"You're truly in your own world, totally self-sufficient and cut off from everything else. You won't miss the evening news because it will have absolutely no bearing or effect on our little world, yet you'll find yourself hovering over the single side band radio to catch the high seas forecast which you've probably never even heard of."

Tory thought for a second, "I'm excited. I am, but I'd be lying if I didn't admit that I'm also nervous. I just hope I don't mess up. It's all so new for us I hope we can do it."

"I know. I get nervous too right before a long trip. It's a big ocean out there and this is a small boat. As to messing up, I doubt you will. If you do, it's my fault anyway. I'm the Captain, remember. I won't ask you to do anything I don't think you can handle. If I do, I will have failed at my job and it means I made a mistake in judgment, right?"

Tory leaned over and gave him a warm kiss on the cheek that lasted a little longer than a peck, then pulled back with a big smile. "What's the plan for tomorrow?"

"Let's all meet here as early as you can get the kids ready and we'll take a little shakedown sail out in the bay in the morning and then do our food shopping and stowing in the afternoon. After that we should all get a good night sleep and see if we can't get out of here first thing the next day. Sound like a plan No. 2?"

"Yeah, it does." Tory gave Ryan another quick kiss on the cheek and climbed back onto the dock before driving away. Ryan returned to programming waypoints in the GPS. He worked till about 10:30 and then after helping Clifton up on the dock they went for a short walk before retiring. A half hour later he was in his bunk relishing the gentle motion of the boat and fell soundly asleep minutes later.

Rip Converse

Chapter 4

The White Lady lay silent and drifting halfway between Great Abaco and Mayaguana in the Bahamas chain. She was sideways to the sea and slowly rolling from side to side. All four of her main engines and both generators had dieseled to a halt some two hours earlier and since then White Lady had been laying broadside to the large ocean swell rolling under them from the coast of Africa some 4,000 miles away. From the onset both Manuel and the engineer had been below in the stifling engine room trying to locate the source of the problem. Edward had initially been unconcerned at their mechanical problems but his patience with the engineer had waned in the last hour and he'd joined them below. The three of them were making little progress as they fumbled in the 110-degree heat and darkness of the engine room.

"You stupid fuck! Am I the only man on this cockroach of a vessel with a fucking brain? How complicated can this be? None of the engines are getting fuel. Obviously, the problem has something to do with the primary fuel filters or the main feeder line from the tank. I swear, if you don't get these engines running in the next fifteen minutes, I'll fuck you up so badly that your cock-sucking mother won't recognize you!" Edward screamed.

Manuel was using his body as a buffer of sorts between Edward and the now trembling engineer under the pretense of holding the flashlight for the terrified man. "Senor Edward, Jorge seems very close to solving the problem. Why don't you go up on deck where it is cooler and get some fresh air? I will stay below here and help him."

"Don't patronize me Manuel. I pay this fucking brain-dead moron $85,000 a year for his 'expertise'. And I don't think he could change the spark plug on my fucking lawn mower!" Edward turned and paced several times in the small area between the engines and his demeanor suddenly shifted from that of homicidal rage to one of seemingly harmless amusement and he chuckled to himself.

"Wait a minute, I don't even own a fucking lawn mower. How could he change the spark plug on my lawn mower when I don't even own one?"

"Yes, that is true Senor Edward. Good point. Perhaps if you went up on deck and had some fresh air and a cool drink, he could better focus his attention on the problem. I am sure we will have it fixed in a short time."

Edward hadn't had any of the coke that he was becoming increasingly dependent on in the previous hour and decided that Manuel was probably right, some fresh air and a few lines of magic dust might improve his outlook on the situation.

"Alright Manuel, but I'm serious, if this motherless son of month-old ejaculate does not get these fucking engines running within 15 minutes, I'm going to send Paulo and his knife down here to do a little dance with him. Do you comprende my inference you dumb spick?"

Manuel nodded his head. "Si Senor." Since their departure from Sippican on the New England coast six weeks earlier, Edward's crack and coke consumption had increased, and he was frequently awake for days at a time. His temper was often violent, and Manuel had little doubt that he was serious. All he could hope for was that they were able to fix the engines or at the very least determine the cause of the problem in the next quarter hour.

"It will be so Senor Edward."

As soon as Edward left the engine room, Manuel leaned closer to the engineer. "Don't worry Jorge. I am sure you can find the source of the problem and we'll be underway in no time. I will keep El Jeffe off your back until you complete your repairs."

Although Manuel spoke with a soothing confident tone, Jorge knew Edward's threats were not idle ones and that his life depended on his being able to solve the problem before Edward returned. Three months earlier he'd seen Edward completely lose it and beat one of the deckhands to death with a peening hammer.

Every kilo of coke that they transshipped was carefully weighed out on a laboratory type scale before it was delivered to them with the weight clearly marked on each package. The now dead deckhand had been foolish enough to think that taking an ounce or two for his own personal use would never be missed. After all, he reasoned, they carried dozens of kilos at a time. Unfortunately for him, as Edward's dependence had increased, so too had his paranoia and obsession with the drug, and it was not uncommon for him to frequent the area where the drugs were stored several times a day, just to be with it, touch it, and reassure himself by its presence. It was on one of these trips he noticed that the seal had been broken on one of the packages. He weighed the package with his own digital scale confirming his suspicion that it had been tampered with. Unsure as to who the thief was, he had called all the crew together in the engine room for an inquiry of sorts and made a big show of weighing out their cargo, brick by brick, pausing after each one to look over their assembled faces. His ploy worked and by the time he got to the short kilo, the guilty crewmember panicked and attempted to run from the room. Edward had a short ugly peening hammer at the ready on the table next to him and when the guilty party broke from the group, Edward had thrown the hammer squarely into the man's back. While this alone should have been enough punishment (as he crushed several vertebrae with the blow), Edward decided to make an example of the man and proceeded to smash each of his fingers and toes, his major joints, and finally his skull. The engineer still vividly recalled the sound of the hammer as it smashed into the man's body over and over and the man's screams. While Edward beat the deckhand, he'd carried on a strange one-sided dialogue with the eventually unresponsive man.

"So you want to dance with Edward? Well how about a dance with Mr. M.C. Hammer? Can you get down? Dance with this you, motherfucker!"

By the time Edward finished he was in a complete psychotic rage and covered in the other man's blood, bone and fecal matter; an object lesson not lost on the rest of the crew.

Chilled by the memory the engineer redoubled his efforts. He'd in fact narrowed down the source of their fuel starvation to the primary fuel feed line, or something in the main tank itself.

"Strange, isn't it? What could possibly have gotten into a line so large to reduce the flow so much?" asked Manuel.

"I don't know. I've never encountered a problem like this before. It is almost always accumulated sediment in the filter or algae growth in the tank that would cause fuel starvation of this magnitude. It's clearly not the filter, nor do I think it could be algae growth as I've have been treating the fuel on a regular basis."

After removing the line altogether and blowing it out Jorge finally came to the realization that the problem must lay within the tank itself. "Manuel, I think there's an access port on the top of the tank although I've never opened it. I'll crawl back there and see how far into the tank I can see. There must be some type of debris that has found its way in there."

Manuel crossed his fingers as the engineer crawled back into the confined space that housed the primary fuel tanks. They were already hours late for their rendezvous and Edward was sure to be uncontrollable when he returned from the main deck if things were not fixed. Unbeknownst to them the source of their problem was a Juicy Fruit gum wrapper that had been dropped into the tank by a careless welder five years previous. In the vessel's five-year history of operation, the small piece of foil had floated around harmlessly within the tank until this particular day, and as it nudged up against the screen in the fuel tank, the fuel rushing around it had opened it to the point where the foil effectively cut off the flow of fuel into the main lines.

"Manuel, pass me a plumbers snake." Jorge requested.

Manuel returned with the snake and passed it through the crawl space to the engineer.

"I don't know if I can dislodge whatever is in there, but if I am able to open the blockage you should see an immediate flood of fuel to all of the filters."

Jorge fished around the interior of the tank with the snake but was unable to locate the source of their problem. He finally gave up after five minutes and bolted the access plate back onto the tank and crawled out.

"What the hell am I going to do?" he asked hysterically. "I'm running out of time and I know that sick prick was serious!"

Manuel could feel the engineers panic and tried to think what they could possibly do next to get at the source of the blockage. "I have an idea. What if we attach a compressor line to the hose right before it runs into the tank and blow pressure through it? Might that work?"

"Yes, that might work, although I hope we still have pressure in the compressor tank. It's been several hours since the pump last ran. Let's try it though." The engineer hurried to the other side of the machine space and looked up at the pressure gauge on the compressor and smiled. They still had pressure. Manuel again did as directed and within two minutes they had the compressor hose hooked up to the main line. It was at that moment that they heard the watertight door slam at the entrance to the engine room.

"You cock suckers better have some good news for me." Edward was back, with Paulo the ferret standing behind him. The engineer looked back anxiously, his eyes darting nervously back and forth between Paulo and Edward.

"Yes, Senor Edward, as a matter of fact we do." As he spoke Jorge motioned to Manuel to send a blast of pressure through the hose into the tank. Simultaneously he looked around the area he was in for a good place to slam his head against. He had no intention of being conscious for his own demise if his last efforts failed. They all listened to the compressed air making its way into the main tank and then a bubbling sound from inside the tank. Jorge stopped the air flow and withdrew the nozzle from the fuel line. Immediately fuel started pouring out of the hose and onto the deck-plates. He smiled and quickly slid the end of the hose over the nipple that led into the primary filters and all four of them watched as the glass fuel bowl in the first filter rapidly filled.

Manuel smiled and reached out and patted Jorge on the back. "Good work, I knew you would find the problem."

Edward was not as impressed and simply said, "How long till we are underway?"

"About 10 minutes Senor Edward. All of the engines will be air-bound and I will have to bleed the first engine I start, cylinder by cylinder to get it going. After that one is started, I will simply backfill all of the others using the fuel pressure of the diesel return line. Yes, I think 10 more minutes should do it."

"Just do it." Edward gave him one last pointed look and turned away making his way out of the engine room leaving a sneering Paulo behind.

"You came this close 'amigo,'" Paulo warned. He held his thumb and index finger a half inch apart.

Manuel turned to Paulo's pitted face. "Get the fuck outta here you little slug before I step on you."

Paulo stood staring into Manuel's eyes for a moment before leaving. "You and I Manuel, soon."

Within 15 minutes the White Lady was underway again at 28 knots, the embolism gone from her fuel lines. Edward stood in the wheelhouse alongside the captain, alternatively checking their GPS position against the chart and staring into their long-range radar screen with the sweep set to 24 miles. It was important that they rendezvous with their supplier, load, and be underway again in the four hours of remaining darkness. They'd only be exposed for a relatively short period of time when they loaded the cocaine but it was important to be gone and out at sea again at first light as the U.S. Coast Guard and Navy had this particular transshipment area under close surveillance by planes, turbine helicopters, ships and a host of satellite imaging devices. Although not as heavily surveilled as the Straits of Florida or the Windward Passage between Haiti and Cuba, this area was still closely watched due to its proximity to the Florida coast.

After they picked up their load, they'd then steam northeast directly for Bermuda away from the U.S. coastline and the more heavily traveled routes smugglers typically took. After making landfall in Bermuda and a stay of several days, they'd file a float plan for the Chesapeake area and then off-load to a smaller fishing boat before clearing U.S. Customs in Annapolis, Maryland. The benefit of traveling the more circuitous route being that private yachts arriving in U.S. waters from Bermuda were not generally examined as closely by U.S. Customs.

Much of the water in the Bahamas is extremely shallow and the Captain was drenched in sweat as he piloted the White Lady the last five miles of their approach to the small island they were headed for. Already shallow at 20 feet, the depth shoaled down to 15 feet for the last several miles. White Lady drew 12 feet and even a glancing contact with the jagged coral beneath would render her dead in the water if she came in contact with any of it. And although there was a channel of sorts marked with day marker poles, they were running the ship dark on the off chance that there were other ships in the area. They didn't want to risk using the 600,000 candlepower searchlights mounted on the wheelhouse roof for fear of betraying their position. Hank, the captain, deftly piloted the large ship at full throttle through the obstacle-course-like channel using only radar as a guide.

"We are coming up on the final turn Senor Edward. Would you like me to head straight in or shall we hold outside?"

Edward had no reason to suspect that anything might interfere with their transaction as he'd made this same pickup on four other occasions, but his basic nature was cautious. "Hold, just outside of the cut into the lagoon, Hank. I want to make sure the rest of the crew is ready."

Hank backed off on the four large CAT diesels as Edward quickly tapped out two large lines of coke onto the chart table and snorted them into the back of his nostrils with the large gold tube he always carried. He took a moment to savor the pleasure/pain sensation as the harsh chemical impacted the sensitive tissue in the back of his nose and then exited the wheelhouse down the ladder and walked out onto the main deck where Paulo, Manuel, the engineer and two deckhands anxiously stood checking their weapons as best they could in the almost complete darkness.

"Manuel, you and Paulo stand by with me to go ashore in the Cigarette. You other three stay alert and patrol on deck. After we make sure that everything is as it should be ashore, we will signal you and you can drop the hook then. If we do not signal within 60 minutes, steam immediately out of the lagoon and hold outside in the channel." As was customary in the trade, Edward would first inspect the product, and only when he was comfortable with the weight and quality would he return to the White Lady and tender payment.

Edward gestured to Manuel to lower the boat from its cradle on the deck above into the water then took the flashlight that Paulo was holding, aimed it towards shore and turned it rapidly on and off three times. After a pause of several seconds the signal was mirrored back from shore indicating that things were still a go.

"Manuel, pass me my Mack." Manuel passed it to him and Edward deftly smacked the bottom of the clip on the Mack 10 to make sure it was seated correctly and racked the charging handle on the stubby little weapon chambering a round.

"All right gentlemen, let's see what our friends have for us." Edward swung a small canvas bag containing a testing kit and a portable digital scale into the Cigarette before climbing in. Paulo and Manuel held the smaller boat off the stern of the White Lady while Edward turned over the engines. They shattered the still night with their poorly muffled staccato rumble. The island they were using for transfers was owned by the Bahamian government and leased to their Colombian supplier. With the exception of the dirt airstrip carved out of the palms and the small finger pier to which they were headed, it was featureless and uninhabited except on nights when a transfer was taking place. Edward slowly maneuvered the Cigarette alongside the dock. Paulo and Manuel crouched prudently low, their weapons at the ready as they approached. One of the figures on the dock turned on a flashlight and illuminated the edge of the dock.

"Hola, Senor Edward. We were beginning to wonder if you had gotten lost. Please, come ashore. We must conclude our business as quickly as possible so that we can all get out of here before daylight," the figure on the dock holding the light shouted out to him.

Edward recognized the speaker immediately as an upper level employee of the cartel whom he'd dealt with during his first transaction two years previous. He was immediately suspicious, as they did not normally send someone as highly placed as Juan without a reason. Edward was correct in his suspicions. As with the initial transaction, Juan had been sent along to garner impressions of Edward's competence and state of mind and to then report back to his superiors. They had received a negative report on Edward's increasing drug use from Mr. Slade after the incident in Massachusetts weeks before. His suppliers preferred to terminate "loose cannons" rather than risk a premium off-loading location such as the island they were on. If Edward's behavior impressed Juan as being erratic and/or unstable, he was under instructions to kill him.

"Hola back to you Juan. Como esta usted?"

"I am well. Thank you for asking. Have your men throw up your lines up and we will get started."

Although the two men accompanying Juan were armed, the initial tension felt by all had been lessened by Edward and Juan's cordial greeting and his men dropped their ready stance and let their weapons hang by the straps as they received the lines tossed up by Paulo and Manuel. They quickly secured the boat and Edward climbed up onto the dock. After Edward and Juan shook hands the six of them made their way down the pier to the dark palms that came right to the edge of the lagoon. They all felt comfortable using their flashlights as they made their way over the dark makeshift path emerging several minutes later at the edge of the palms where an ancient DC3 stood silently on the dirt runway. Juan opened the rear door and motioned for Edward to accompany him in. He followed him up the short ladder and stood just inside the door as Juan went forward to the cockpit to turn on the interior cabin lights. Edward was temporarily blinded by the lights as they came on, but his eyes adjusted quickly and took in the carefully wrapped and stacked bricks of cocaine; just over 180 kilos.

"Very, very nice Juan. It always takes my breath away to be surrounded by so much power."

"Yes, quite so. Shall we begin then?"

Edward knelt on the floor, unzipped his small canvas bag, and removed a small rack of test tubes, several bottles of chemicals and a knife that he used to make small punctures in a series of the bricks. One by one he tested small amounts, being careful to draw them in a random fashion from the bricks of blow surrounding him. After testing each sample he weighed the brick it had been taken from and compared his scale weight to the weight printed on the top of the sample brick. As he'd expected, they had slightly different purity levels as they had been manufactured on different days and sometimes at different locations, however all tested out between 82 to 88 percent pure which was within the agreed upon limits and the weights tallied. Each brick had the distinctive red wax seal of the supplier.

"They all look good Juan. What's the total weight of the shipment?"

"Four hundred pounds, as agreed. To be precise it came out to four hundred and three pounds, four ounces, and 3.955 grams including packaging materials. Is that acceptable?"

"Yes, that is fine."

Juan reached over to one of the pierced packages. "Perhaps you would like to have a taste while we have it open?" Juan tilted out almost a gram onto the top of one of the bricks. Edward desperately craved a line but he resisted and casually reached over and took only a small amount on the end of his finger which he then ran along the insides of his gums.

"Thanks Juan, but I prefer to keep a clear head while doing business. Besides, we must be careful, this shit can be habit forming." Edward had an uncanny ability to sense danger and he knew he was being watched closely for his reactions. After his meal with Mr. Slade in Massachusetts he knew he was on a probation of sorts and these were people he'd no desire to get on the wrong side of.

"Very well, as you wish. Why don't we have our men begin transporting the goods down to the dock and you and I can go out to the boat and conclude the transaction."

"Sounds good to me."

They emerged from the fuselage of the DC3 and each gave instructions to their respective crews reminding them that they only had two hours left before daylight and walked off together down the path to the Cigarette. Before firing up the engines Edward used his light to signal the OK to his other crew on the White Lady and after receiving back the agreed upon signal he and Juan idled out to the ship as she dropped anchor several hundred yards off the shore. Keeping one crew and the captain on board he ordered the remaining crewmember and the engineer to take the Cigarette back ashore to help with the loading and took Juan up to the main salon where they'd complete the financial end of their deal.

Major distributors and the cartels had discovered years before that it was physically impossible and impractical to use cash for deals of this magnitude and as a result had devised a simple method of transferring escrowed funds using trusted intermediaries. The intermediary in this case was on Grand Cayman. All that was required was for Edward to indicate his assent and the amount in combination with a pre-agreed, one-time only code. Edward picked up the satellite phone on the end table with Juan looking on and dialed their intermediary's number on Grand Cayman.

"809-294-0022, may I help you?"

"Yes, this is echo, delta, whiskey, 5556988. Please transfer funds in the amount of $8,000 as previously arranged." Edward had deleted the last three decimal places of the amount mentioned on the off chance that their conversation was being monitored. The smaller amount would not raise the eyebrows and interest of eavesdroppers the same way $8,000,000 would have.

"May I speak with the other party please?" The flat voice on the other end asked. Edward passed the phone to Juan.

"Yes, this is Juliet, uniform, alpha, 2327272. I agree."

"Very well, the funds are released and will be credited to your account in the morning. Thank-you for calling."

Edward placed the phone back in the cradle. "It is so much easier nowadays don't you think?"

They walked out onto the afterdeck of White Lady as the Cigarette returned with the first load. Jorge was driving accompanied by one of the deck hands. They quickly tied off to White Lady's stern and began carrying dozens of the plastic wrapped bricks through the watertight door that led into the engine room. Edward and Juan climbed down the short staircase that led to the stern and joined the two men below in the engine room.

Beneath the steel gratings of the engine room floor White Lady had been retrofitted with a new stainless-steel water tank that had not been a part of her original design. The engineer busily stacked the bricks through a large rectangular hole in the top as quickly as they passed them to him. The tank looked exactly like the other two water tanks on the ship, accurate in construction right down to valves at the base and feeder lines that fed into the ship's water main. But this tank was also equipped with a small interior holding tank full of water. Even if they were to receive a particularly thorough Coast Guard inspection and someone pulled the feeder line off the valve, water would come out when it was opened. The only access into the tank was the opening through which Jorge was now stacking their cargo. It would be welded closed after they finished loading effectively sealing the tank from any standard inspections. When they reached their final destination, they'd simply use a torch to cut the plate off. This was a far safer system than the one they'd employed on previous trips where the product had been stored behind a concealed panel at the front of the engine room.

"This is a good system Edward," remarked Juan.

"Yes, I think so too. Someone would have to be very good to find the product. I was a little worried about cutting the plate off with a torch at our destination and burning up all the product, but I came up with a solution for that. Once the cocaine is loaded, we simply cover the product with asbestos blankets before welding the top back on."

Edward turned to his men. "I want this entire area washed and scrubbed with diesel fuel after the loading and welding are done; every square inch between the stern and this area, comprende?" The two men nodded their assent.

"And wait for the steel plate to cool before doing it, eh? We don't want any fires. After you're done cleaning the area put some grease on a rag and rub it over the top of the whole tank. Then sweep up some dirt and filings off the machine shop floor and blow it all over the surface of the tank. I don't want some suspicious Customs agent asking questions about the fresh welds on the top of the tank."

Edward and Juan ascended the short stairway back up to the level of the fantail and emerged into the quiet night air where they smoked and watched the flashlights of the men ashore who were moving out of the palms and up onto the small pier where they stacked the rest of the load. The loading was complete after just an hour.

Edward addressed his crew on the stern as the Cigarette was lifted back into its cradle. "I want to get underway immediately and be clear of this area in 15 minutes."

He pointed to one of the deckhands. "Marco, you go forward and raise the anchor. The rest of you make sure the Cigarette is washed as well as the rest of the boat. You ready to depart Hank?" Hank nodded.

"Let's do it then."

Hank fired up their four main engines one minute later and the White Lady was underway three minutes after that and heading back out of the small channel to sea. Edward headed off to his stateroom and his freebase pipe.

Rip Converse

Chapter 5

Ryan had planned on rising early, but the gentle sea breeze coming in through the hatch and the sound of the water lapping against the hull had worked like a narcotic on him and he didn't awaken until he heard the excited chatter of Tory, Jan and Willy as they boarded the boat at seven the next morning. Tory came below first and then helped Willy down the stairs.

"What's this?" Tori asked. "I thought you'd be standing in the cockpit with the engine running and cursing the day you met us. Instead you're sound asleep as though this was just another day. Well it isn't, so get your lazy butt out of that bunk and let's get moving! We have people to meet and things to do today."

'Jesus this woman is beautiful.' Ryan thought to himself as Tory staged her little faux tirade.

"Well, are you just gonna lie there and stare at me all day like I'm some sort of beauty queen, or are we going to get moving?" Tory pounced on the end of his bunk and straddled his still inert body leaning down close to his head with hers and pinning his arms with a huge smile on her face. The sensation of Tory's warm legs around his stomach felt wonderful to Ryan.

"You are, you know." he said in a quiet voice so the kids wouldn't hear.

"I'm what?"

"A beauty queen."

"You are so brain addled. Did you fall out of your bunk and hit your head last night?"

"I'm just stating facts, girlfriend."

"I don't believe our relationship yet warrants that title."

"I'm just sayin."

Willy sidled over to the edge of the bunk hearing their whispering. "What's going on mom?"

"I'm just trying to think of a way to get our lazy Captain out of bed. Got any ideas? Mine don't seem to be working"

"We'll just tickle him?" Willy suggested quite matter-of-factly. Jan was looking on now too; and although she didn't say anything, Ryan could tell from the smile on her face that he was about to be triple-teamed.

"And out of the mouths of babes," Tory noted with a delightful smile.

She ground her crotch into his stomach and impishly said, "I don't think the lazy swab is worthy of our attentions, but a good tickling just might straighten him out." All three simultaneously attacked him through the blanket, laughing hysterically. Ryan squirmed and bucked trying his best to evade their attentions but finally yelled "uncle" and broke free of their grasps throwing the blanket off and retreating to the back corner of the bunk, daring any one of them to come within his now unrestrained grasp. Ryan had no shirt on.

Tory make a quick faint with her hand and Ryan instantly grabbed her by the wrist, swung her around, and pulled her to his chest using her body as a shield against the children. She was warm and soft although still resisting and he tightened his bear hug around her front until she stopped. He'd pinned her arms to her sides, one forearm across her stomach, the other across and between her breasts. The children suddenly disappeared from his consciousness and he found himself aware only of her freshly washed hair, soft neck and hard little breasts. He realized it had been weeks since he'd touched or been touched, and it felt good. As Ryan tightened his grip, Tory gave into his strength. It felt wonderful to be held by a strong pair of arms and she leaned back compliantly into his chest. It felt so natural, the way he held her, his casual near nakedness, as if they'd been close and together for years. In a flash the last few years of her struggle with drugs and alcohol and subsequent year of hard work at recovery washed over her leaving a deep sadness in its wake. Willy and Jan sensed the change in their mother's mood and instinctively backed off.

Willy finally interrupted their moment, "Well, are we going or are you guys going to play kissy face all day?"

66

Jan echoed his sentiment. "Yeah guys, enough with the "you know what." I thought we were going sailing this morning."

Without anyone noticing, Tory casually wiped her misted eyes and pulled herself back together. "You're absolutely right kids, enough delays and shabby excuses from this poor excuse of a captain."

"Alright, alright. You win!" Ryan swung his legs off the bed and ran a hand through his tousled hair. "Let me make some coffee and get dressed. Then we'll go sailing."

Ryan got dressed and made coffee while Tory and the kids helped Clifton off onto the dock and then they brought their duffels and the casseroles Tory had prepared below. Willy and Jan immediately began unpacking their clothes and personal items into the drawers under their bunks. As everyone settled in, defining their space in different ways, Ryan sipped his coffee and wondered again at his instant family and sudden loss of privacy. A blessing or a curse? He still hadn't decided.

When they finally cast off at nine, the sun shone brilliantly in the crisp, azure, fall sky and the wind was blowing about 15 knots from the northeast. Ryan navigated them out of the small channel and into the outer harbor. He turned to Tory. "Why don't you take it?"

Tory had sailed before, but all her previous sailing time had been in small sailboats like Lasers and Sunfishes. She'd no experience handling a vessel of Parthenia's size. Noticing her hesitation Ryan said, "It's really no different than the smaller boats you've sailed, it's just a little slower to react to the helm. Steer a straight line between our present position and that red nun about a mile off our bow." Ryan pointed over her shoulder to the buoy that lay off in the distance.

Tory slipped in between Ryan and the binnacle as he spoke and took the wheel. Ryan stood behind her for a minute or two to reassure her by his presence then went forward to attach the halyard and remove the sail ties from the mainsail, leaving her in the cockpit. Willy and Jan looked on with rapt interest at their mother steering the boat. Ryan noticed their wavy path through the water as he looked aft at their wake but was pleased Tory hadn't been hesitant at taking the helm. Overall, she was averaging a good course. He knew she'd be a perfectly competent helmperson in no time. He turned back towards Jan.

"Jan, you see that rope wrapped around the winch in the center of the cockpit near your knees?"

Jan looked up startled. "Yeah."

"I want you to untie it from the cleat and then unwrap it from the winch." Jan looked at her mother with a questioning look as she tentatively reached over to follow Ryan's instructions. She'd just assumed that because she was a kid and didn't know anything about sailing that there wouldn't be an active role for her on the trip. She was fearful and excited at the same time that she might play some type of an adult role. She followed his instructions, freeing the main sheet, and Ryan hoisted the mainsail aloft.

After setting and trimming the mainsail Ryan went below and pushed the #2 jib up through the deck hatch from the forepeak and then he hanked it onto the forestay, hoisted it and then returned to the cockpit to trim the sail and sit with the rest of his crew. He shut down the engine and everyone was momentarily silent as they drank in the sensation of Parthenia making her way effortlessly through the light chop under sail power alone. They didn't travel far that morning. Instead Ryan kept them quite local and focused most of their attention on sail handling, tacking and man overboard procedures.

"Alright, listen up for a few minutes guys because what I want to go over with all of you is really important. The single biggest danger to any one of us, is the possibility of falling overboard when we're at sea. Even under the best of circumstances in small seas, in daylight, it is very easy to lose someone if they fall overboard. At night, it's next to impossible." Surprising everyone, Ryan grabbed a small cockpit cushion and threw it overboard.

"Now, these are ideal conditions. I want you all to pretend that the red cushion rapidly disappearing in our wake is me. Here's what you'd do. First, whoever is steering yells "man overboard" as loud as they can, then immediately throws the man overboard pole and ring over the side along with anything else handy that floats. Next, note your exact compass course mentally and continue to steer it and simultaneously press this button on the GPS repeater at the helm station (Ryan pointed to a button on the remote readout of the GPS that was arranged among the instruments on the binnacle). When you press this button, your exact location at the moment you press it, is put into memory. That way if you do lose sight of the person you can find your way back to that area. As soon as you have someone else on deck I want that person to go forward and let go the halyard on the jib. When that is down, the helmsman should reverse course 180 degrees and start back on the reciprocal course with everyone's eyes on the water. The man over-board pole has a bright orange flag that flies about six feet off the water and there is also a bright strobe light that turns on automatically when you throw the pole over the stern, so look for those. If and when you find me, turn the boat up into the wind when you get to me so the mainsail luffs and the boat stops. Then throw me the end of one of the jib sheets so I can pull myself aboard. Got it?"

"Jan, you come forward with me a minute so I can show you where to let go of the jib halyard. Willy, your job is to stay back here in the cockpit and to keep your eye on the cushion."

Jan went forward with Ryan and he showed her how to let the tension off the halyard and then drop the sail. After dropping the jib onto the deck, he yelled back to Tory to tack the boat around and Jan and he returned to the cockpit to lend their eyes to the search for the cushion.

After about 15 minutes Ryan called an end to the search. Even though the sea was only running two to three feet, they were unable to recover the bright red cushion.

"I hope you all remember me fondly," Ryan joked. "And I hope you all got my point, because those cushions are expensive. The easiest way to avoid being lost at sea, is to never fall over. So, whenever anyone comes on deck, particularly at night, be careful, and anyone leaving the cockpit should wear a safety harness! I don't want to lose any of you."

Ryan's object lesson was not lost on his assembled crew and no one talked for a few minutes as each one of them thought about what it would be like to go over at sea and not be found. Ryan let the lesson sink in and then started the engine for the brief run back into the harbor. He had Tory take the helm again and asked Jan to help him drop the main and fold the jib. He wanted all of them to be as familiar as possible with raising and lowering the sails.

As he and Jan tied off the sail bag with the jib in it, he looked her in the eye.

"You're doing a great job Jan."

She blushed shyly and averted her eyes.

"Is there anything else you want me to do Ryan?"

He was somewhat surprised by her helpful attitude and quickly thought of things he could have her do to encourage her interest. Subconsciously, he'd expected Jan would be of little use as a crew and had just assumed she would listen to her headphones, read, complain and generally act as most 12-year-olds. Her enthusiasm made him aware that he really didn't know either child as a person.

"Yes, there is. Back behind your mother there's a small hatch called the lazarette. I keep all the fenders and dock lines in there. Pull out the four lines that are on top and the three big rubber fenders underneath and bring all of it amidships on the port side. Do you remember which side is port?"

"Yup, it's left, right?"

"You got it. After you get all that stuff up on deck, I'll show you where I attach the docking lines and how to hang the fenders."

Jan went aft and started fishing the docking gear out of the lazarette as Ryan had requested. Tory was as surprised as Ryan at her helpful attitude. Since they'd been reunited, Jan had been more withdrawn and quieter than before their separation. Tory knew that part of it was adolescence, but she also knew that there was a lot of anger and insecurity festering not far below the surface due to Tory's year-long absence in treatment and the halfway house. To the child in Jan, Tory had abandoned her and her brother and she knew it would take a long time to regain her trust. Tory smiled down the deck to Ryan as Jan went about her chore, glad for the positive interaction between them and the possibility that the trip might offer Jan some identity and power over her negative self-image.

They passed through the harbor entrance and entered the main channel. Willy was the first to notice that there were several police cars, a fire engine and a large crowd gathered on the dock. "Mom, look at the police cars!"

Ryan looked up. "It looks like someone got hurt. I can see them carrying a stretcher up the gangway from the float." He and Jan tied off the last of the fenders and Ryan returned to the cockpit and took the helm from Tory. They motored alongside the pier and Ryan yelled up to one of the old timers. "George, what happened?"

"Hey Ryan." He reached down to take the proffered spring line from Tory. "Don't really know. Brad was out tending his pots this morning and came across the body of some dead woman floating out near Keel Shoal. Nobody seems to know who she is, but it seems as though she was hurt real bad before ending up in the drink."

Tory threw the other lines to George and he dropped them over the various piling heads that Ryan pointed to. Ryan shut down the engine, then properly tensioned each dock line before turning to Tory. "I'm going to see what I can find out about this woman. Why don't you get the kids ready and then we'll head to the supermarket as soon as I'm done."

"Ok. I'm not real anxious for them to see any more than they have, so give me a shout when they've finished." Tory replied.

Ryan vaulted up onto the pier and went over to the edge of the crowd. The ambulance attendants had just finished loading the woman's body and were shutting the rear doors of the ambulance when Ryan arrived at the edge of the crowd. He went over to one of the policemen.

"Scott, what happened? Was it anyone we know?"

"Hey Ryan, I'm not really sure, she's pretty decomposed. No one's been reported missing from around here and she's been in the water for some time, so it's difficult to tell." Scott paused. "She was naked and tied up and not so old by the looks of it."

The ambulance drove off several seconds later and the crowd started to disperse. Ryan went back aboard Parthenia and related what he'd learned to Tory. "No one seems to know who she is or what happened to her. In any case we can take the kids up now and go to the supermarket if you're ready?"

"We're ready when you are. How strange though. Has anything like this happened before here?"

"Not to my knowledge, although I'm sure there will be a big investigation. My friend Scott said that the woman was naked and tied, which doesn't sound much like a swimming accident."

Tory thought for a moment and wondered at the horror of being thrown naked and bound into the ocean and wondered if the woman had been conscious when it all happened.

"She was probably just part of a drug deal gone bad up the coast and drifted down here." Ryan said.

"I'm sure you're right but it makes me feel strange that this happened right as we're leaving."

Ryan locked up the boat and then all five of them piled into Ryan's truck and headed off to the local Shaw's supermarket to load up on the canned goods and other supplies that would sustain them for the first two legs of their trip. The passage to Bermuda was typically only four or five days but it was Ryan's plan to buy quite a bit more food than they needed as it was so expensive in Bermuda and the Caribbean.

It took them almost two hours to do the shopping. Jan and Willy particularly enjoyed being able to pick out virtually all the junk food and candy they wanted as Ryan and Tory methodically went down their lists picking out essentials. They filled four shopping carts to overflowing. At checkout their total came to nearly $1,400.

"Where on earth will we put all this stuff Ryan?" Tory asked.

"Don't worry, it'll fit. The main thing is that we put it all away together so we both know where everything is. We'll also mark the tops of all of the cans with the contents of each with Magic Marker."

Jan and Willy ran ahead to the truck and climbed up onto the bumper to pet Clifton. Without even being aware of it, Tory and Ryan each put an arm around the other as they followed across the parking lot.

"Ryan, I don't know what's going to happen over the next few weeks or months, but I want to thank you again for letting us come along. Are you having any second thoughts?"

"Not really. It feels good to me too. Anything that feels this good couldn't be wrong even if you are a bit of a wise-ass at times."

Tory knew he was kidding and pulled a little closer before separating and going to the passenger side of the truck. They swung the truck around to the loading zone in front of the supermarket, loaded the groceries and then returned to the boat to stow everything. By 6 p.m. they'd finished and Tory decided to take the kids back to the house for a bath and early bed while Ryan topped off the water tanks and finished up last minute details. "See you first thing in the morning guys, sleep well," Ryan said.

"You too," Tory replied and kissed him warmly before heading up the ladder.

None of them slept well that last night on shore due to the excitement of their impending departure. Ryan was up by four, Tory and the children by 5:30. Bill and Stephanie had agreed to let Ryan keep his truck at their house and after the short drive up to their house at six and tearful exchanges between Tory and Stephanie, the four voyagers waved a final goodbye and walked through the quiet pre-dawn streets each lost in his or her own private thoughts. Even Willy who normally had a question or comment every few moments, was silent as they walked back through the village.

Ryan was feeling anxious and somewhat overwhelmed by the responsibility he was taking on. He was quite comfortable with the pace of the relationship that had been slowly developing between Tory and himself, but the whole concept of children and the innocent reliance they tended to bestow through simple familiarity made him break out in a cold sweat whenever he thought of himself cast in the role of surrogate parent. In the past, extricating himself from relationships had been relatively easy because most of his previous partners had been single. With kids he knew it would not be so easy. Quite simply children seldom had any ulterior motives and he was scared that if he allowed them to get too close, he would lose his only avenue of escape, their indifference. If he let them get close and decided later to leave, he would have to confront his own inadequacies.

Tory wondered if she was making a sound decision for herself and her children. Did she really need to sail off to the Caribbean to re-establish their relationships and to have them end up in a healthy, stable environment? Both children had already made new friends in Sippican, they were away from the city and already in a community of basically good people. Deep down she suspected that her willingness to go south with Ryan had recently become more about her own selfish needs and she wasn't feeling comfortable with herself as a result. She almost brought the whole issue up with Ryan as they got to the end of the dock but it was a bit late for that now. Then Bill and Stephanie rolled up behind them just as they got to the boat.

"I know we already said our good-byes back at the house but we just didn't feel right about you guys taking off without a proper goodbye."

Tory was touched, and in conjunction with her earlier thoughts found it impossible to hold back more tears. "You've both been so good to us the past month and a half I don't know how we can ever really repay you."

"When you get settled in whatever tropical paradise you find we'll come down and freeload off *you* for a few weeks. That's fair, right?" responded Stephanie.

"Anytime." she replied with a loving look at the two of them.

"Don't get so maudlin Tory," Stephanie said trying unsuccessfully trying to keep back her own tears. Both Bill and her hated to see Tory and the children leave. They'd given up trying to have children of their own years before and had gotten quite close to Willy and Jan over the preceding six weeks. They had known Tory through good times and bad since childhood, so it had meant a great deal to see Tory putting her life back together. Stephanie would especially miss Tory's optimistic energy and their late-night talks.

Ryan was anxious to leave. He thanked Bill and Stephanie again for their help and support, gave Stephanie a hug and Bill a handshake and hurried onto the boat to start the engine. When they finally slipped their lines and pulled away from the dock the mood had gotten only sadder, and Bill and Stephanie's parting words were, "Let us know if we can ever help, in anyway." And "Call us as soon as you get there!"

Ryan wondered to himself where in-fact "there" would be and felt at this moment as though both he and Tory were "running away from" rather than "running to" something in particular. Bill and Stephanie watched and waved for several minutes as Parthenia steamed out of the harbor and into the early morning dawn before getting back into their car. "I hope they'll be all right," Stephanie said to Bill.

"Me too," he agreed.

Chapter 6

Tory curled her cold, wrinkled toes into the teak grating she was standing on, as much for balance as to reassure herself that they were still attached to her feet and re-adjusted her grip on the wheel. She'd only been on watch since midnight, but the two hours felt longer. Thick, dark, pregnant clouds now filled the horizon to windward totally obscuring the moon, giving the night a spooky quality. And even though there was nothing to see in the blackness behind the boat, she found herself periodically looking over her shoulder. They were 500 miles offshore, in 3,600 feet of water, out of the shipping lanes on a dark and increasingly stormy night; and she was the only one awake. The feelings of isolation were profound.

She cracked her neck from side to side and hunched deeper into the protection of her foul weather gear before raising her eyes from the compass to peer across the cockpit and down into the cabin. It was softly illuminated by a single infrared bulb at the chart table providing just enough light to see Willy and Jan's sleeping forms in the main cabin bunk to leeward. The preceding three days had been difficult for them both; especially Willy, who had been seasick from the moment they had left Cape Cod. Right beneath them on the cabin sole, Clifton slept as best he could, shifting position every few minutes as he tried to find a comfortable position within the tilting confines of the small cabin. Big dogs are totally unsuited to travel at sea. He suffered the indignity and obvious discomfort with only an occasional groan. He was very much an integral part of the crew.

A sudden gust shifted her attention back to the compass and she realized that it was taking more effort on the wheel to maintain their magnetic course of 162 degrees. The dimly lit anemometer in her instrument cluster indicated that the wind had risen another 5 knots in the last hour and was holding steady now at 20 mph with gusts to 25. She suspected they might have to reduce sail soon but decided to wait another few minutes to see if it would hold steady. She didn't want to wake Ryan unless it was necessary. This was their third night at sea and his first one below in a bunk. The first two nights he'd slept on deck in the cockpit in his foul weather gear during her watches while she got the hang of steering a compass course and became acclimated to night sailing. He knew that his physical presence would be reassuring to her. She'd appreciated it at the time but now wanted to show that his faith in her as a helmsman had not been misplaced and that she wouldn't panic at a little extra breeze.

Below, Ryan lay curled up in the aft quarter berth directly below the starboard side of the cockpit, alternating between the coma his body craved, and the half-awake/half asleep fitful rest his mind would allow. Lying there, he kept thinking of Tory. No matter the depth or difficulty of the distractions that he'd faced in the weeks preceding their departure, the moment his mind was not specifically focused, challenged, or otherwise directed, it invariably wandered to her and the children, much the way water seeps into a hole dug at the ocean's edge. Sweet, mysterious Tory: fiercely independent and self-sufficient, yet tender and vulnerable at the same time. To date, their physical contact had been limited to small passing touches and their intimacy to a close familiarity that came from working closely towards a common goal. He'd been content to just be with her and savor the dichotomy of her personality rather than rushing into an intense, short-lived, sexual experience that was the norm for him.

He also knew that she was completely devoted to Jan and Willy, a relationship that was almost symbiotic. The three of them came as a package deal. He also suspected, from the way she jealously guarded and protected them, and the way they seldom left her side, that there was more to their family history than she'd chosen to share with him so far. He wondered if the roles were reversed whether he would have been up to the challenge of raising two children alone and slid gratefully back into his comatose state without an answer.

On deck Tory fought an increasingly strong windward helm with the waves frequently washing down the leeward side of the deck. The anemometer now indicated a steady 24 knots of breeze with gusts to 28. Tory was suffering from a false optimism and paralysis that often afflicts helmsmen on dark nights; if they wait just a little longer, the wind will calm some and it won't be necessary to wake everyone to reduce sail. If you're skirting a passing squall it's often possible to change course and trim slightly and accomplish this alone, but she did not yet have the experience to differentiate between a passing squall and an approaching front line, nor did she have the confidence to alter course and trim sail on her own. If she'd gone below during the previous hours to look at the barometer, she would have seen that the pressure was falling, rapidly, indicating more than just a passing squall. But she hadn't.

The first indication Ryan had that something was wrong was Tory's scream as Parthenia rounded up into the wind. The wind spilled from the sails, the boat came quickly upright out of her 20-degree heel and the sails started luffing, the crisp Dacron luffs of both the main and the jib cracking back and forth in the escalating wind. Ryan woke up immediately and launched himself out of the bunk to the companionway stairs and slid back the hatch not knowing what to expect on deck. He quickly assessed the wind, sea and sky and knew they had to head off the wind and reduce sail immediately or run the risk of shaking the rig apart. The blackness on deck was total except for the instrument and compass lights and the phosphorous kicked up by the boat pounding into the oncoming waves. Conditions had decayed dramatically from when he'd turned the helm over to her at midnight and he cursed himself for not having acted on the harbinger of high thin clouds that had been moving in as he went below. He should have taken a reef before going below.

He rushed up the companionway ladder into the cold night air and yelled to Tory to turn the boat away from the wind and pointed downwind. Bending over the genoa winch he started to ease the sail out as the boat started its turn downwind.

"What's your course now?"

"185 degrees," she yelled back.

"Take her down another 30 degrees." Tory continued to turn the wheel and watch the compass. Ryan slackened the mainsail along with the jib as they came off the wind. Within moments the boat was moving through the water once again at a good clip with the wind now aft of the beam. Once Tory was settled on the new course Ryan climbed up behind her and stood on the lazaret hatch with one hand gripping the backstay. From this vantage point he could see how well she was able to steer the new course he'd given her and better assess the overall conditions. He also knew it must have scared her the moment they rounded-up into the wind and he wanted to reassure her that things were again now under control and that she was doing a good job.

She steered the new course with rigid determination, convinced that she'd almost killed them all. He watched their course for several moments and then leaned close enough so he didn't have to yell.

"Why didn't you wake me earlier before the wind increased so much?"

"I did! I stomped on the floor over your head for almost five minutes like you told me to, but you didn't hear me!"

He leaned down and put his arm around her shoulder. "I'm sorry, I must have been really out. We'll work out a better system in the morning. Can you stay on the helm for a few more minutes while I get on a harness? We're going to have to get back on course and I need to reef the mainsail to do that."

Tory nodded yes, and Ryan went below to get a safety harness and flashlight. He also wanted to check on Willy and Jan who were both anxiously peering over the webbing wall he'd rigged to the outside edge of their bunk up to the cabin ceiling to keep them from falling out of the bunk they were sharing. "You guys OK?"

Their two shy, tousled heads nodded yes. "Is Mom OK?" Jan asked.

Ryan smiled down at both of them reassuringly. "Yeah, she's fine. The wind just got a little stronger since you went to sleep. I'm going to take some sail down so we can be more comfortable."

He got into his safety harness then reached behind the companion-way ladder to the central switchboard and flipped on the overhead spreader lights. Instantly the mast and foredeck of Parthenia were illuminated. The lights would make his job of reefing the mainsail easier. The downside was that Tory would have to concentrate harder on steering an exact compass course as the bright light would ruin her night vision and make compensation for wave action more difficult. He reached over the cockpit combing and clipped onto the lifeline that ran fore and aft along both sides of the deck. Before heading forward he explained to Tory what he was going to do and what was expected of her. "The most important thing for you to do is keep a steady course and stand ready to make adjustments when I yell them back to you. Ready?" She nodded and he stepped out of the cockpit onto the deck and crab-walked up the windward side holding the cabin roof-rail as he went. He used extra caution as he moved. Tory had learned a lot over the previous days, but he knew there was little chance that she'd be able to manage the boat alone and less that she could return to find him if he did fall overboard in the current conditions. When he reached the base of the mast, a cold, stinging rain started and quickly soaked him. Still dressed only in his underwear he muttered an expletive as goose bumps quickly rose on his near naked skin and he bent to untie the main halyard and lower the mainsail several feet to the first reef point.

Tory looked up from the compass every few seconds to check on his progress. When the rain began and started pelting her in the face and eyes, she lowered the visor on her foul weather gear another inch. "What the hell am I doing here?" she wondered. When she'd originally asked Ryan if they could all accompany him, she'd had visions of soft trade winds, hot sunny days and exotic fruit drinks in tropical, out of the way anchorages. This was anything but that. She trusted Ryan and his judgment, but the natural forces present were intimidating and underscored their total isolation from the outside world.

Ryan realized they'd have to head back up into the wind several degrees as the main was still too full to pull the tack of the sail down far enough to slip the reefing ring over the hook on the gooseneck. He yelled back, "Tory, bring her back up into the wind 10 degrees."

Tory put her hand to her ear signaling that she hadn't heard his instruction and he pointed with his hand in a windward direction which she understood. Gradually she steered Parthenia back up into the wind until the main started luffing again. He held his hand up for her to stop.

She assumed correctly that this was the new course he wanted her to maintain and returned her focus to the compass. After securing the new tack point on the reefing hook, Ryan grabbed a winch handle from the deck box at the foot of the mast, tightened the halyard again and turned his attention to the second half of the reefing operation which entailed winching in all the excess sail at the rear or "luff" end of the boom and bringing it down tight. He did this, then standing for a few moments at the base of the mast, looked forward and sized up the sea and wind again. "Better to take another reef," he thought, and reached down to lower the mainsail yet another few feet and again took up halyard tension and winched in the excess luff. He then started to work his way back to the cockpit on the cabin roof using the reefing ties as he went to tie up the excess sail now hanging uselessly below the boom.

Tory watched as Ryan worked. He'd been in such a hurry to get on deck and reduce sail that he hadn't put on any clothes before coming on deck and was still dressed in only his underwear. Tory smiled and critically appraised him in the harsh lights of the spreaders. Ryan was only about 5-foot-10, but he was incredibly fit and it showed in the striation of every muscle as he went about his work. He had large shoulders with lean defined deltoids, a hard, flat stomach, good pecs, sculpted ass and truly great calves, she mused. Tory didn't work out but, in the weeks, leading up to their departure she'd noted his routine of running several miles every other day and lifting weights at the local gym at least three times a week. It showed and his dedication over the years had left him with an enviable physique for someone half his age.

"What am I thinking," she said to herself. "Here we are in the middle of the Atlantic Ocean, in a raging storm, and I can't keep my eyes off this guy."

He looked back towards the cockpit several times as he worked and was aware of her appraisal. He was nearly naked and as he climbed down into the cockpit suddenly felt exposed and self-aware in his wet briefs. He tried to cover his discomfort. "Let's head back up to our original course and I'll trim as you bring her up."

Tory nodded with a smile and slowly brought the boat back to 162 degrees.

"What are you smiling at?" he asked.

"Oh, nothing," she chuckled gently and pointedly averted her gaze in a direction away from him.

Ryan turned serious again. "Can you stay at the helm just a bit longer so I can go below, check our position and maybe get on some *clothes* and foul weather gear?"

Tory sputtered then laughed before nodding. Ryan went below, plotted their position on the chart and then looked up to the barometer to note it in the log. He looked at the earlier barometer notation from three hours earlier. It had fallen substantially in the short period. He also checked the wind speed again on the anemometer and noted that it had risen to a steady 30 mph and was now gusting to 35. 'This is going to get a lot worse before it gets better,' he thought and went forward to dig the small storm jib out of the sail locker. In all the years he'd owned Parthenia and the dozens of trips south he'd made, Ryan had only had to use it a handful of times. On the last occasion, the wind had peaked at 72 knots with seas as tall as the masthead and at the height of that storm they had taken a knockdown and the three-burner stove had broken free from its gimbals and nearly killed a close friend who was asleep in a bunk across the cabin. The heavy stove had shattered his friend's shoulder and caused considerable damage below before they were able to wrestle it into a corner and tie it to the mast. The next day they had him airlifted off the boat by the Bermuda Coast Guard.

With that in mind and before going back on deck, he made a thorough check around the cabin to make sure everything was stowed and dogged properly, including the lids on the battery boxes and the heavy propane stove in the galley. He hoped they didn't have a repeat of the storm he'd endured several years ago because it was sure to terrify Tory and the kids, but he'd every confidence in Parthenia's ability to weather anything short of a hurricane. After checking on the children, he pulled on his foul-weather gear, grabbed the storm jib and climbed back up the ladder into the black night.

"Tory, I'm going to replace the No. 3 with a smaller storm jib."

She looked up at him. "Do you really think we need to?"

"The barometer has fallen a lot over the last few hours and there's a good chance it's going to get worse. With us shorthanded I'd rather make the effort now while I can still work the foredeck. Can you hang in there for another 15 minutes?"

She was shivering from the damp and cold and dead tired, but she nodded yes. Ryan snapped into the lifeline again and grabbed several sail ties and started working his way forward, dragging the bagged storm jib behind him. The seas were breaking over the bow with increasing frequency and he knew it would take longer than usual to get things squared away. He secured the storm jib to the base of the mast, then worked his way back to the cockpit and had Tory bear off the wind some more and eased the sheets accordingly. He figured they'd probably take less water across the deck on this point of sail and went back forward to drop the No.3. Manhandling it to the deck, he rolled it forward to the bow, tied several sail ties around it, unclipped the hanks, then dragged the whole sodden mass back to the cockpit. Normally he would have dropped it through the forward deck hatch, but with the seas they were taking decided against it. One good-sized wave through the forward hatch could take them straight to the bottom. He rested for only a moment before heading forward yet again; this time to hank the tiny storm jib onto the forestay and to raise it. The only sail reduction left was to take a third and final reef in the main or lower it altogether. As they came back on course he felt a little foolish because their speed had dropped from 7 knots to just 3 knots and they were now underpowered for current conditions. But experience told him he'd made the right decision and he decided to wait things out and see if the storm developed over the next few hours. He set the Aries self-steering vane, turned and put his arm around Tory. She was still shivering. "Are you hungry?"

"Not for food, but I could drink something warm and I'd like to check on the kids."

"Ok, we'll both go below and I'll make some coffee. You can change into warm, dry clothes."

Tory pointed nervously to the Aries self-steering vane. "Can we really trust that thing to keep us on course?"

"For short periods on this point of sail, but I have to overhaul it when we get to Bermuda. I think it has a lot of salt built up in the gears."

Tory nodded, but really didn't understand the self-steering vane. Ryan told her before leaving that it would make their lives simpler, but it had been temperamental and ill-mannered since the first day and she didn't trust it.

Ryan went below first, dragging the wet No. 3 jib up into the forward cabin. Then he started a pot of coffee in the coffeemaker and knelt down and petted Clifton as Tory explained to the children what it was like up on deck. When the coffee was ready, he filled two mugs and after passing one to Tory, sat down at the single side band radio to listen to the high-seas weather forecast. Tory clambered over the webbing into the large bunk the children were sharing and read them a story as she drank the hot liquid. Clifton made his way over to Ryan's side of the cabin and curled up at his feet under the chart table.

The high seas forecast for their area east of the Gulf Stream called for winds up to 55 knots from the northeast and 25-foot seas. A gale center had formed up off the coast of Hatteras and would pass directly over them during the next 12 to 24 hours. Ryan compared the broadcast position of the low with their position and realized there was a good chance they'd face much steeper, breaking seas as the wind built. He was glad he'd made the sail change when he had. Clifton whined several times as he made his 4 a.m. log entry and after Ryan finished what he was doing, helped him up the ladder and into the cockpit after attaching a lead to his collar. Once outside in the enclosed area of the cockpit Clifton gave him a disgusted look and lifted his leg against the inside. Not a fire hydrant, tree or wheel rim, but after eight straight hours below what's a dog to do? Clifton climbed back up to the companionway entrance and let Ryan help him below again.

The wind increased steadily over the next two hours and Ryan watched with dismay as it rose past 45 knots. He found he had to trim the sails every few minutes to keep them full because as it increased, it was also clocking around to their beam. As the wind increased, so did the seas, and it was a wild world he beheld as the sun slowly rose out of the east. By 6 a.m. it was gusting to 55 knots and even with the wind behind them, a storm jib and three reefs in the main, they were overpowered.

"Tory, I need you up on deck!"

Tory was feeling seasick after laying in her bunk below. With all the hatches and portholes closed the air was fetid. Normally quiet below, the noise and violence of the storm that raged outside easily penetrated Parthenia's hull, making sleep impossible except for short catnaps. Sleep was also made more difficult by their excessive angle of heel and the jarring crashes that shuddered through the boat as waves slammed into her side. In many ways she felt even more tired than when she'd come below from her earlier watch just from the physical effort of trying to stay in her bunk. She was awake when Ryan called down to her and got out of her bunk, opened the hatch several inches, and peered out. Ryan was back at the helm with his legs spread wide for balance and head slightly down to deflect the wind and spray.

"How're you doing?"

He smiled before replying. "It's getting pretty bad up here and I need you to take the helm while I take in the rest of the mainsail. Do you feel up to it?"

She didn't but nodded her head yes anyway.

"Good. Get on some gear and don't forget your harness," Ryan yelled above the maelstrom.

She went over to Jan and Willy's bunk to check on them and let them know she was going back on deck. "We have to get some more sail down. You doing OK?"

Jan nodded. "I guess."

"This storm can't last forever. We've been through worse stuff on shore anyway right?"

Jan knew what she meant and just nodded.

"Good. Keep an eye on your little brother and I'll be back below as soon as I can. Love you." Tory leaned over the nylon webbing that kept them from falling out of their bunk and gave her a kiss on the forehead.

"Love you too, Mom. Be careful."

Tory had taken longer than she meant to with Jan and rushed into her foul weather gear and safety harness. She knew if she stopped too long to think about what it was like on deck she might lose her nerve and when she finally slid back the hatch and crawled out into the cockpit, it was worse than she'd imagined. The wind had risen another 5 knots to

60 and was starting to blow the tops right off the waves. "What do you want me to do?" she yelled nervously.

"The same as last night," Ryan shouted back, "First we'll come up into the wind some and I'll trim as we go. Hold the course I give you and I'll go forward and get the rest of the mainsail down. We're starting to take some waves in the cockpit now so make sure to clip your harness onto the binnacle and keep a good grip on the wheel!" Tory hesitated a moment building her courage.

"Don't worry. You'll be fine as long as you're clipped in," Ryan yelled, sensing her nervousness.

Tory took a deep breath, eased herself the rest of the way into the cockpit, and clipped herself to the binnacle.

"Wait a minute for your eyes to adjust to the darkness," Ryan shouted. She did as he suggested and braced herself next to him for a minute or two before reaching for the wheel.

"I'll be OK now."

Ryan nodded and turned the wheel over to her. She immediately started a slow turn back into the direction of the wind. He prepared to move forward. The turn increased the wind coming over the deck and now instead of running with the waves, they'd be going into them again. They started taking large swells over the bow that roared down the deck. Ryan tried to time his departure from the cockpit to move forward between the larger sets of waves. When he judged the time was right, he gripped the starboard lifelines in one hand and the cabin top rail in the other and crab-walked quickly forward. He stayed low to reduce the body mass he exposed to the oncoming waves. Despite his caution, twice his feet were swept out from beneath him leaving him hanging precariously by his arms. The waves would then slam into the cockpit combing, become airborne and drench Tory in spray and backwash. The cockpit drains at her feet quickly became overwhelmed at the volume and before long Tory was up to her knees in water, the cockpit full of hundreds of pounds of seawater. She watched Ryan struggle down the deck and realized with new and sudden clarity how totally dependent she and the children were on him. Her faith in him and his abilities had been complete to this point, but the scale of the forces present in the howling wind and hissing waves was eclipsing that trust. For the first

time, Tory felt truly scared and was weak-kneed as she watched him
work his way forward to the relative safety of the mast. Everything was
out of scale. The boat which had seemed so large and strong out of the
water, now felt hopelessly inadequate. The wind, which had been their
silent ally only hours before, now threatened to tear their sails and
capsize them as they climbed to the top of each wave and were exposed
to its full fury. The seas were mountainous, each wave thousands of
tons. Her thoughts turned to the life raft still securely lashed forward of
the cabin house. The thought provided little comfort with the knowledge
that it was only about a twentieth the size of Parthenia when inflated.
She turned her head forward to check on Ryan's progress, but even
breathing was difficult as the wind and spray tore at her face. The next
time she looked up Ryan had reached the relative security of the cabin-
top behind the mast and was facing aft towards her. His face was in
shadow from the overhead spreader lights, but it almost looked to her as
if he was smiling. He stood there for several moments with his arm
hooked around the mast getting his breath and at one point tilted his
head back and looked up the mast. His face was momentarily
illuminated, and she could see that her earlier impression had been
correct. "What on earth was there to smile about?"

Ryan let off the main halyard and brought the sail down the last few
feet. Immediately the boat's motion through the water was smoother and
more upright. After tying the halyard off to a cleat on the mast he began
working his way aft along the cabin roof holding onto the boom and
wrapping sail ties around both it and the excess sail to secure the loose,
hanging sail material. Anything left unsecured would flail in the high
winds and eventually tear if were not tightly tied. Parthenia's motion
through the water was much smoother after the sail reduction and Tory
breathed a short sigh of relief. The storm continued to batter them, but
she felt they had regained some measure of control over the boat.

Ryan stayed on the windward side of the boom using it to lean against
as he tied the sail material to the boom. Normally a simple operation,
the seas they were in made it far more difficult than normal.
Compounding this was the lack of any mainsail aloft. The boom was
now free to swing from side to side as they rolled in the troughs of the

waves. If there had been another crew aboard, they would have taken up the excess main sheet slack before Ryan tied off all the reefed sail. But there wasn't and he instead hung on to the heavy boom as best he could as he worked his way aft. As he approached the cockpit he leaned over the boom to tie the last sail tie and smiled down at Tory conveying that the job was almost complete.

Tory smiled back nervously. Suddenly a large irregular swell slapped the side of the boat causing a pronounced and unexpected roll. When the wave hit, Tory had her eyes glued to the compass. Rather than looking up immediately in response to the boats shudder, she instinctively ducked her head in anticipation of the wall of water she knew would follow. One came, as she'd expected, and she kept her head down for a few extra seconds as the water washed over her and into the cockpit. When she did finally raise her head, Ryan was gone.

Tory looked again to the area on top of the cabin where he'd been standing only moments before and blinked repeatedly as much in denial as to clear the saltwater from her eyes. Everything slowed and she became hyper aware, not only of her physical reality, but also of her own thoughts. The wet, aluminum wheel suddenly felt colder as she gripped it with white knuckles and the wind howled through the rigging above her head. She closed her eyes as if that might help her to find some hidden inner courage or a refuge from the unthinkable.

Another large wave slammed into Parthenia and Tory reflexively dipped her head and shoulders again into the oncoming spray as it washed over the cockpit. She kept her eyes closed for as long as she dared as if it was in her power to deny what had just happened. But she knew she had to look, if not for her and the children's sake, most certainly for Ryan's. She opened them. There was no longer any doubt about it. Ryan was gone, he'd been washed overboard.

The boom that he'd been hanging onto for support now swung freely from side to side in great long arcs above the cabin roof with the mainsheet tackle hanging from the end of the boom.

Tory wailed out a long "Nooooo!" and immediately tried to remember all the things Ryan had told them to do if one of them fell overboard. She knew Jan would never hear her cries of "man overboard" if she yelled and she didn't want Jan on deck anyway. She remembered the GPS and quickly found and pressed the button on the GPS repeater to record their position and tried to think what Ryan had told her to do next. The man overboard pole, that was next! If she could get that free and into the water perhaps Ryan would somehow be able to make his way to the strobe beacon and bright orange flag attached to it and given a little time to think, she might be able to turn the boat around and make for it herself. She reached frantically behind with one hand and started to fumble with the strap that secured the horseshoe shaped float in its quick release bracket. This in turn was connected to the white strobe light, and man overboard pole by a line. If she could just get the strap unsnapped, throw the ring over, and pull the pole out of its sleeve on the backstay she knew that the strobe attached to it would automatically turn on as soon as it floated upright. She also knew it was important to get it over the side as soon as possible because it would be next to impossible for Ryan to swim any long distances in the heavy sea; especially dressed as he'd been in his foul weather gear and sea boots. His chances for survival were poor at best, and every passing second reduced his chances as Parthenia surged forward. Tory struggled to find the release behind her. She knew in her heart that no one could stay afloat in such a storm dressed as he was, and her movements became desperate.

"Goddamn it!" she yelled into the night. She felt totally helpless, overwhelmed and suddenly very guilty that she'd failed him and decided in desperation to let go of the wheel and use her flashlight. When she did, Parthenia immediately came up into the wind, paused with her luffing storm jib shaking the rigging, then fell off again on her own, and kept up the same sequence. At least 20 seconds had already passed and they were probably hundreds of feet away from him already. The violent luffing threatened to shake the rig apart, but at least she wasn't broaching or tacking over with the helm left unattended. Using both hands she quickly got the life ring out of its bracket and focused exclusively on freeing the rest of the apparatus and throwing it over the side. The strobe activated immediately and illuminated the surrounding ocean in a bright white light every two seconds.

"Tory, Tory! Turn up into the wind!"

At first she thought she'd imagined the sound and swept her flashlight in an arc over the deck of the boat. Ryan was nowhere in sight. Then she heard his cry again and she was able to determine that his cries were coming from under and behind the boat! She leaned out over the side catching a flash of foul weather gear red in her peripheral vision and leaned out further still. Ryan was in the water dragging by his harness under the stern counter desperately trying to keep his head above water by hanging onto the tether. Even though he was still attached to the boat by his lifeline, their forward motion through the water threatened to drag him under and drown him in the next few seconds if she couldn't get him aboard. She knew he couldn't possibly have much strength remaining and spun the wheel to windward. Parthenia quickly turned head to wind, the storm jib filled on its back side and the boat came to a complete and unexpected halt in the water. Tory had inadvertently put them in "irons" and the boat was dead in the water for the moment.

She grabbed onto Ryan's lifeline where it was still attached to the safety line and with almost the same maternal strength that she'd have found within if one of the children were facing imminent death, she somehow pulled his heavy wet form close enough alongside so that he was able to get first an arm up over the side and then a leg up over the gunnel where he hung, half on the boat, half off. The trunk of his body was still outside the lifelines, but Ryan could go no further for several seconds. Eventually, scared that one of the large waves rolling past them would sweep him from his precarious perch and back into the water he finally rolled his body inward of the lifelines and onto the deck where he lay, gasping for air and unable to speak for several minutes. Tory burst into tears of relief and started hugging and kissing him, and then just as suddenly, began hitting and yelling at him.

"Goddamn you Ryan! How could you? When I looked up and you were gone I ..."

"I know, I know," he replied and pulled her into his arms. She still didn't know whether to laugh or cry but settled on just hugging him back as well as she could through two layers of foul weather gear and their tangled safety harnesses. After a full minute of rocking back and forth in the tangled mess, they disengaged. The boat was still in "irons" and traveling backwards slowly. Ryan was concerned that a wave might throw them back onto their own rudder which could snap the shaft.

"We need to get up and get moving forward again."

They both stood up and he looked at the boom, still swinging from side to side. He wanted to get them underway in a forward direction again as quickly as possible. Before heading off the wind he grabbed onto the block and tackle hanging from the boom.

"Tory, I want you to steer again for a minute while I get the boom in and belay it. Can you do that?"

"No! Just leave it. Can't we just go below and wait for this to end. I don't want to lose you again."

"Tory, I have to. Don't worry, nothing will happen."

She continued to hold him and looked him squarely in the eyes. "I'm scared."

"I hope so! If you weren't, I'd wonder about you. Anyone with an ounce of sense would be but we have to get the boat under control again."

The power of his confidence, and simple logic of mind over matter cut through her fear for the moment and she nodded.

"Ok, but I swear, if you fall over again, I'll kill you. Please be careful," Tory took the helm back from him.

"If I fall over again, you won't have to." In truth, Ryan's trip into the water and dragging behind and underneath the boat was the closest he'd ever come to death at sea and he wasn't anxious to go there again. After retrieving the main sheet tackle that hung from the boom and getting it belayed, he winched the boom in amidships and they got back on the correct tack and headed in the general direction of Bermuda, although Ryan's main goal at this point was to find a safe heading and point of sail in degrading conditions. He would have pointed them back towards Massachusetts if that would have provided a safer motion through the water, but the safest course also happened to be in their favor and after getting Tory on the best course he turned to examine the main sheet block where it had let go from the traveler to see if he couldn't determine why it let go. He knew the hardware was rated for a much greater load than had been placed on it and looking over the fitting at the base of the block he noted right away that nothing had broken. The 1/4-inch Monel pin that went through the base of the lower block connecting it to the traveler car had simply fallen out. Normally the pin was kept from falling out by a tiny circular cotter pin. All he could figure was that the back and forth swinging motion of the boom had somehow worked the cotter pin loose. One little, tiny pin was responsible for his fall overboard and he looked down into the water sloshing around inside the bottom of the cockpit to see if it was there. He shook his head in wonder when it glinted back at him from the scuppers. He looked over at Tory and realized how lucky all of them had been that she'd been able to get him back aboard. Although her lower lip was still trembling, she'd performed with a clearer head than most.

"Tory?"

She looked up from the compass.

"Thanks for saving my life," he held up the small pin that had fallen out of the primary main sheet block.

"That's what's responsible?"

He smiled and nodded.

"I guess now's a good time to tell you I'm sorry…"

"Sorry for what?"

"For throwing your nice shiny, light and man overboard ring and pole over the side for no reason."

Ryan turned and looked at the bracket where it customarily hung and thought about it for a second. "Good for you, you remembered. Let me rephrase that. Thanks for saving my life, but next time just make absolutely sure I'm really gone before throwing $1,200 of safety gear over the side. I'm just messing with you. You did everything perfectly. I'm sure we can get another setup like that in Bermuda or have one air freighted in."

The waves continued to break over the boat and into the cockpit almost continuously and Ryan took the helm back from Tory to give her a break. "Why don't you go below and get some rest. I can handle it alone for a while."

"You sure?"

Ryan nodded.

Tory crawled through the tilted cockpit, slid back the companionway hatch and made her way down the ladder. She quickly shut the hatch behind her to keep out any of the now constant flow of seawater coming over their deck and cabin top. She got out of her wet gear and crossed the cabin to Jan and Willy's bunk. The smell in the small cabin was foul. Both kids had been sick to their stomachs. Willy was asleep, but Jan's eyes opened as she sat down on the edge of the bunk and Tory put a hand on her forehead. "How're you feeling?"

"Not too hot. I tried to make it to the toilet before I got sick, but ..." Jan felt guilty and embarrassed at the mess on the floor.

"Don't worry about it sweetie. I'll clean it up. You want something cold to get the taste out of your mouth."

Jan nodded and Tory made her way back across the cabin to get her a boxed fruit drink and some paper towels to clean up with. As Tory wiped up the vomit off the cabin sole she had to struggle to keep from getting sick herself. She drank a juice box and then climbed over the lee cloth into the same bunk with the children. After getting settled, she lay there listening to the wind shrieking through the mast and rigging and to the massive waves as they roared down the deck. She'd never heard anything like the pounding sounds as waves crashed over the bow and then ran down the length of the deck. The sound of the wind going through the rigging alternated between mournful and shrieking.

Ryan felt as though he was drowning on deck. The wind continued to rise and was now blowing a steady 65 mph with gusts to 75. The seas had become steeper and were breaking almost constantly over the boat. He knew the almost square waves were occurring because they had crossed into the Gulfstream and the wind was blowing against the 5-knot current. With the breaking seas, the rain, and the tops of the waves blowing right off, it was a near liquid environment. He knew he wouldn't be able to stay on deck much longer and began debating the best way to heave-to.

He'd been in similar wind conditions on several occasions before, but had never dealt with such severe, breaking seas. He was reluctant to throw out a sea anchor unless there was no other choice. To do that he'd have to first take down the storm jib which would involve another trip to the foredeck, and he decided to first see if Parthenia could be persuaded to sail by herself with the self-steering vane. No matter what their course, however, the salt clogged gears kept sticking and it couldn't be relied on to hold a steady course. He had another idea and started experimenting with trim tab and rudder settings as an alternative to the Aries. The trim tab that ran the length of the trailing edge of their keel had a manual brake that was located on the binnacle, and after engaging that he planned on tying off the wheel with a piece of line if he could get her to hold a steady course. After several tries, he found a heading quite close to the wind where Parthenia would stay in balance on her own. She was making forward headway and keeping a consistent wind angle even when some of the larger waves would pick them up and throw them into the trough of the next wave on their side. Parthenia would recover each time and then resume her heading.

Below the children were leaning against Tory snoozing fitfully. She gently eased their heads to the pillows before climbing out of the bunk. She was dry and feeling more secure now, despite the conditions outside and wanted to stick her head out of the hatch to check on Ryan and see if there was anything he needed. Just as she got to the ladder, she heard a metallic crashing sound from the forward cabin and turned her head to see what had fallen. In absolute horror she watched as seawater poured into the forward cabin from the ceiling. She wrenched the companionway hatch open and screamed at Ryan, "There's water pouring into the forward cabin, what should I do?"

Ryan was momentarily speechless as he ran the possible causes through his mind. Had one of the anchors stored up forward broken free and punched a hole in the side or had they maybe hit some half sunken object? Neither scenario was good, and something had to be done immediately but he hadn't finished securing the helm yet.

"Run forward and see if you can tell how it's getting in."

"OK!" She yelled and after sliding the hatch closed again made her way forward. She could see immediately upon entering the cabin that the source of the water was through the deck plate that the chain for the anchor passed through as it came up out of the chain locker. She remembered that normally there was a metal cap over this hole on deck and figured that the cap must have been wrenched off by a wave sweeping the deck. She also remembered that there'd been a small lanyard attached to this plate to keep it from going over the side and wondered if it were still attached. Regardless, she knew she'd have to crawl into the small, dark, confined space to find out. She ran back into the main cabin for a flashlight, hurriedly returned then started pulling sail-bags onto the cabin floor which were blocking the small opening into the chain locker.

Jan was suddenly beside her. "Are we sinking?" she asked in near panic.

"No, I don't think so, but I have to crawl up into the chain locker to find out what's wrong. I think the deck plate that covers the anchor chain hole came loose. Can you hold the light for me?"

Jan stuck out her hand for the light. "Want me to look? I'm smaller and can get up in their easier."

"That's OK, you just hold the light," Tory answered impressed with her daughter's courage. She crawled across the double V-berth and up to the opening that led into the chain locker. It was an oval shaped hole about 3 feet tall, by 1 ½ feet wide. She paused for a second as Jan shone the light ahead of her. Seawater continued to cascade downwards through the deck hole and had already filled the chain locker to the point where it was now running freely over the 3-inch lip of the oval opening and washing over the V-berth cushions and onto the floor of the main cabin. Tory hated small spaces but crawled ahead regardless, the possibility of sinking a compelling motivator. Jan followed her as far as the opening and shone the light in and upwards. Due to the volume of saltwater that poured into her face and eyes every time she turned her head Tory couldn't see much. Jan could however, and guided Tory with her voice.

"The rope is to your right Mom!"

Tory felt in that direction and as soon as she located it, followed it up with her hand through the deck hole. She pulled herself further into the locker until she was sitting atop the pile of chain and maintaining a downward pull on the lanyard with one hand and feeling around with the other up through the hole. She located the aluminum cap right away. 'Thank God. It's still attached.' She thought to herself and began trying to get it back in place. Every time she got close, however, another wave would crash over them and throw her sideways into the oak frames of Parthenia's skeletal frame and she would lose her grip on the cap as she was thrown across the compartment. She gritted her teeth against the pain.

Jan could see how difficult it was. "You've almost got it mom. Try again."

Jan's encouragement helped and after repositioning and bracing herself, Tory waited for a lull between waves. When it came she shoved her arm up through the hole all the way to her elbow and was finally able to get a good enough grip on the cap to pull it into place. The flow stopped immediately, and as long as she kept a downward pull on the lanyard, it stayed in place. Tory was wet and bruised all over. She lay atop the wet chain and paused to catch her breath and take a silent inventory of the bruises she'd sustained. Every part of her hurt and she wondered what she would look like in a few hours. Jan continued to hold the light and shine it into the locker as Tory looked for a place to tie off the lanyard. She finally found one and after securing it Jan helped her out of the small compartment.

"You OK?" Jan asked.

"I don't know. God, every part of me hurts."

"Let me look," Jan shone the flashlight up and down Tory's arms where she'd suffered the worst. The skin was broken in several places and large black and blues had already started to rise. She winced in sympathy.

"I'll be OK, but I should let Ryan know what's going on." She went aft to the companionway and slid the hatch open.

"It was only the deck cap for the chain locker and I was able to tie it off. I don't think it'll come loose again."

Ryan breathed a sigh of relief and yelled, "I found a way to stabilize her and I'm coming below."

"How can you?" Tory yelled back. "Who will steer?"

"No one," Ryan replied. "I've been playing with the trim tab and I think I can get her to sail herself, just give me a few more seconds." Ryan had already tied off the wheel so that it couldn't move, and after making one last correction to the trim tab setting, he screwed the damper down tight and took his hands off to see how well she did on her own. It seemed to work. She was making about 3 knots of forward headway on a course about 80 degrees off the wind with just a slight luff in the storm jib and holding steady. He stayed on deck for several more minutes to make sure she stayed on course then climbed down the ladder into the cabin sliding the hatch closed behind him. He was surprised at the squeaking sound his wet, sea boots made on the ladder as he descended and stood motionless at the bottom of the ladder for several seconds savoring the relative peace and quiet. The maelstrom above was just a muffled roar inside the security of the cabin and his body and senses that had been pummeled for so long on deck needed to reorient. He listened as a can of coffee rolled back and forth in the bottom of one of the food storage lockers, to two mugs clinking in the sink and the stove moving gently back and forth on its gimbals. Across the cabin his entire crew sat huddled in the leeward bunk with looks that varied from sick to expectant. He suddenly felt very guilty.

"How's everyone doing?" was the best he could manage as he peeled off his wet gear.

Tory vocalized the groups feeling. "'Hi guys, how's everyone doing?' Are you kidding? Here we are in the worst storm in the history of the planet and all you can say is, 'Hi guys, what's up.'"

Ryan chuckled. "You mean we're not one big happy family safely ensconced in the dry, secure bosom of our very own luxury yacht?"

Clifton chose that moment to make a retching sound dogs sometimes make when trying to clear their throat. It broke the tension. On an urban scale of one to 10, things were pretty close to zero. The galley was full of dirty dishes, it smelled like vomit and wet gear and clothing lay scattered everywhere. The wind was at near hurricane strength above them and they were hundreds of miles offshore in a tiny 42-foot wooden boat.

Over the next two hours the wind and seas got worse and when the storm peaked they were enduring sustained winds of 75 mph with gusts to 85. Every other wave delivered them a "knockdown." Parthenia would struggle up one mammoth sea after another, only to reach the top and be blown on her side and hurled back, shuddering, into the trough of the next wave. As the storm raged outside Tory, Willy and Jan braced themselves in one leeward bunk with Tory alternately reading to and catching catnaps with them. Ryan and Clifton did the same aft behind the bulkhead separating the navigator's berth from the rest of the cabin. From there he could also monitor their position and the storm's progress and intensity while keeping a protective arm around Clifton.

By 2 p.m. fewer seas were breaking over them and Ryan could tell that the wind was finally starting to diminish. It was still too rough to venture on deck but Parthenia's motion through the water was once again even and balanced. Ryan noted that their general direction throughout had taken them closer to Bermuda and it now lay only 120 miles to their south.

Tory also sensed the change and carefully slipped out of her bunk without waking Willy and Jan and came aft to join Ryan and Clifton on their bunk. She sat down next to Ryan. "It's finally starting to lessen, isn't it?"

"Yes. I'm only sorry that you three had to go through that," he said guiltily and noticed the bruises all over her arms.

"God, what happened to you?" he asked with concern.

"I got banged up a little when I was getting that stupid chain plate tied down. I'll live."

Ryan put his arm around her and all the tension that Tory had held inside for the previous 14 hours rushed to the surface. She put her head on his shoulder, nuzzled her body against his and began to softly cry. Ryan knew what she was feeling and was himself coming back to the world. For the past 14 hours their physical and mental focus had become increasingly narrow until small things that would normally go unnoticed became the very center of their existence; the precise course steered, the size of a sail and it's trim, the way a sheet is cleated off and finally as finite an object as the small 1/4-inch Monel pin that had almost cost Ryan his life. These things had filled their consciousness to the exclusion of all else, and as they lay in each other's arms in the warm security of the cabin their other senses reawakened and asserted themselves. Ryan brushed a strand of hair from her face and tucked it behind her ear, then kissed her; softly at first, and then with increasing warmth and intensity. She tasted salty and had the musty smell of the ocean on her. The warm skin on the back of her neck whispered to his calloused fingers, and her lips, suddenly hot, wet and swollen, opened greedily to his. He could feel the outline of one of her nipples and the gentle swell of her breast through the cotton of their shirts as she pressed against his chest.

She looked at him and completely broke down.

"I was just thinking of the moment when I thought you'd gone overboard and how totally lost and helpless I felt. All the confidence and faith I thought I'd built over the last year failed. There wasn't a thing I could do and I was totally powerless to control and change what was happening to me and this boat. I also felt as though I'd betrayed Jan's and Willy's trust again. Control's a big issue with me because I was "out of control" for so long, and I swore when I straightened out that I would never *not* be in control again. When you went over the side and I thought you were gone, I felt all the fear, helplessness, and despair that I used to feel before I got sober. I didn't think I'd ever feel that way again. That was more frightening to me than the idea of drowning. And now, well, I don't feel that way at all. I suddenly feel very whole and complete. But that's scary too, because so much of that centers around you. Am I making any sense?"

"More than you know. Especially the part about being scared," Ryan held her gently for a few more moments.

"Tory, you didn't fail last night or today and lose control of yourself, for even a moment. Many people would have. In fact, it was just the opposite. Failure for you would have been deciding to have a few pain killers out of the medicine chest or a couple of quick shooters out of the vodka bottle, or letting your fear paralyze you."

"We have pain killers on board?" she asked. They both burst out laughing. She continued. "I also feel guilty for exposing Willy and Jan to this." She gestured towards the outside. "I feel like I put them in a dangerous environment so that I could indulge my own desires again."

"That may be partially true but you're being too hard on yourself. When you told me you wanted to expose them to different environments and give them an appreciation for human values, I listened. It made a lot of sense to me. Hell, if I'd known we were going to go through this storm I wouldn't have brought you and probably wouldn't have gone myself. It's just one of those things that we have no control over. Hundreds of people make this trip every year and this storm is no different than if you were driving north in your car and got caught in an unexpected blizzard. We can't know or predict what might happen at every juncture of our lives. What we've been through over the last 14 hours will probably be a unique and one-time life experience for you. We didn't choose to sail into this storm. It wasn't even forecasted when we left four days ago! We did the best we could with the information we had so don't beat yourself up because of it."

Willy called out for Tory from across the cabin. He was feeling sick to his stomach again and although Jan had done her best to soothe and quiet him, she was no substitute for Mom. Tory savored Ryan's warmth for a moment more, then sat up on the edge of the bunk. "Duty calls," and kissed him once more before getting up and working her way back to the Willy's bunk.

She reached in, picked him up, and hugged him to her with his head on her shoulder and stroked his head. He felt hot and was still fragrant with the odor of being sick. "It's OK, you poor, little, miserable guy."

"I tried to hold the bucket for him, but he missed a little," Jan said as Tory wiped Willy's chin and shirtfront with a paper towel.

"You did fine Jan. He's just feeling miserable and needs his mom." Tory looked around the cabin and realized they'd all probably feel a lot better if she straightened things up, got rid of the wet clothes that seemed to be everywhere, and they all brushed their teeth. They hadn't showered in four days and between Willy's seasickness and the wet clothes scattered around, it was grim below. After cleaning him up she got both children cartons of apple juice and then set Willy back in the bunk with Jan and started to pick up the cluttered cabin.

Ryan poked his head up through the hatch to check on conditions above and estimated that the wind had fallen to about 45 knots as they slept. He also noted that the seas had lengthened and were no longer breaking on them with any marked frequency. The GPS placed them 85 miles north of the Northeast Breakers buoy. It marked the outermost reefs that surrounded Bermuda. For the last several hours their steered course had been taking them northeast of the island but for every foot they had sailed in that direction, the wind and waves had pushed them sideways two feet closer to the island as it lay directly downwind. As the wind lessened, the tiny storm jib no longer provide adequate forward motion and steerage and Ryan knew he'd have to add additional sail within the hour and get them back on a direct course to the island. He did the dishes while Tory finished cleaning up the cabin and when he was finished took Clifton up on deck to relieve himself. This presented a problem as the swells were still so large, and although Clifton's agility was pretty good for a dog his size, Ryan decided to rig a harness of sorts around his midsection before heading up. He adapted one of their safety harnesses to fit him then got into his foul weather gear and helped the dog up on deck, into the cockpit and then onto the stern area. After he was done Ryan reached into the lazaret for the bucket and sloshed the results overboard. Before taking him back below they sat for a while, both glad to be out in the fresh air, Ryan braced with a foot against the leeward cockpit combing, Clifton leaning against him. After several minutes he got him below again and went over to the bunk where Tory lay with the children. "Feel like helping me on deck again?"

"No, but I will. What do you want to do?"

"I want to get some of the mainsail back up and get us moving again."

Even though the wind was still blowing 40-45, Bermuda now lay directly downwind. With their forward motion factored in, Ryan knew that with the apparent wind would only be 30-35. It was time to add more sail.

Darkness was again falling as Tory joined him on deck and they could see stars through the crisp, vacant skies. The low-pressure area had passed and a high followed it. Tory steered again as Ryan went forward and untied the sail ties on the mainsail and then hoisted it about one third of the way up leaving the third reef in. Then he replaced the storm jib with the #3. Bermuda lay directly downwind from their position so he also rigged their spinnaker pole to the jib so that they could sail "wing on wing." He had Tory come to the new course and as soon as he jibed the jib and got the spinnaker pole angled up to windward from the mast, the boat surged forward with both sails full and pulling. Then he rushed back aft to help her steer. On this point of sail in the still huge seas, steering was tricky, even for an experienced ocean sailor. The challenge, as they surfed wildly down each wave, was to keep Parthenia pointed directly downwind and down-wave without spinning out and rounding up into the wind. Ryan was amazed at how well Tory steered, spinning the wheel first one way and then quickly back the other to keep them on a straight course down the center of each wave. Occasionally he would have to verbally coach her and several times he had to grab the wheel when it threatened to get away from her. But she was a natural and as the hour went on she got better and better at it. When she would catch a wave just right their speed would sometimes surge up to over 12 knots. That was 4 knots faster than Parthenia's hull speed. Typically, after almost cresting one wave, a second larger one would hiss up behind them and as the boat rose to the top of that one they'd catch the greater wind available to them on the top of a wave, the sails and rig would fill with the new wind, strain forward and they'd career down the other side of the wave with phosphorescent rooster tails shooting out from under the stern counter, the bow and hull both cleaving and pushing tons of water and spray to the side. Tory caught one particularly large wave just right and their speed climbed to an incredible 15 knots. She squealed like a little kid, "This is incredible, no, more than incredible; it's better than sex! I don't think I've ever felt so alive!" They surfed down another and carried what felt like several hundred yards on just that one wave. Eventually they were hooting and cheering with almost every wave and Jan stuck her head out to see what all the excitement was about.

"Honey, isn't this amazing?" shouted Tory over the noise. Jan was standing halfway up the companionway ladder with just her head sticking out facing forward. Jan had been below for more than 18 hours and quickly became as enthralled as Tory and Ryan.

"Come on Mom, you can get this one ... yes, yes, alright!" And they'd scream down another one with spray flying everywhere and no one caring about getting wet. After another hour of this, Ryan went below to make coffee, check their position and look in on Willy. He also wanted to run the engine for several hours to charge the batteries as they'd be using all their electronic gear as they made their approach into Bermuda. Willy was standing up in his bunk tentatively peering over the webbing, a little shy, because it was Ryan.

"Hey sport, you want to see what all the excitement is about?" Ryan asked. Still feeling woozy Willy nodded shyly. Ryan reached into the bunk, took him in his arms and went back to the ladder where Jan was still standing.

"Jan, can you come below for a few minutes so Willy and I can stand there?"

She nodded her head and smiled at her brother. "You're going to love this shrimp."

Ryan climbed halfway up the ladder so that both he and Willy's heads were stuck out of the hatch. "Look who I found," Ryan said to Tory. Willy turned aft in Ryan's arms to watch his mother for a moment and then turned forward again quickly getting caught up in the thrill of the ride. After several minutes his color started to return. Ryan was pleased to see him smile and some life return to his face.

"Pretty fun, huh?" Ryan asked. "Feel good enough to eat something?" Willy nodded enthusiastically.

"How about everyone else, food?"

Tory and Jan were also starved, and Ryan returned below with Willy and made sandwiches for all of them. After, he plotted their position and found them just 40 miles from the Northeast Breakers buoy. Ryan poured two coffees and went aloft to share a few minutes with Tory. He put his arm around her as he sat and she leaned back into it, grateful for the warmth and companionship.

"I can't believe how it can change out here. One minute it's quiet and peaceful, then wild and terrifying, and still later, incredibly exciting and almost fun. I don't think I've ever felt so many emotions in such a short period," Tory remarked.

"I know," Ryan replied. He was thinking to himself that's why he'd made the trip so many times over the years.

104

They were silent for the next half hour, caught up in the beauty of the bright moonlight as it played over the leftover storm swells, grateful for the opportunity to be alone with one another.

"How much longer?" she asked.

"I'm guessing we should see lights on the horizon in about three hours, probably another two after that before we get in. No point in both of us being totally exhausted when we arrive. Why don't you go grab a few hours of sack time?"

Tory reluctantly agreed and checked Jan and Willy before stripping off her turtleneck and jeans and sliding gratefully under the blanket in her own bunk. She curled up into a fetal position with her hands crossed between her legs and lay there for several minutes feeling warm and secure and went over the previous 24 hours in her mind before falling asleep. Ryan filled her thoughts.

Ryan sat in the cockpit indulging his own fantasies. He knew their careful, unspoken, restraint was a thing of the past and he no longer cared what the implications were or what responsibilities he might be inadvertently taking on, they simply had to be together. They'd work out the details as they went along.

He woke Tory two hours later so he could go below and manually plot their position on the chart one last time. He also wanted to call Bermuda Harbor Radio.

Tory came on deck.

"Good morning dear," Ryan offered.

"Dear! Well aren't we being familiar with our crew this morning?" She came around to his side of the wheel and planted a warm, wet kiss on his cheek.

"I guess you can call me 'dear' this morning. You're looking pretty 'dear' yourself with four days beard growth and that fancy hairdo."

"Look who's talking! Where did you have your hair done this morning, Burger King?"

Tory sighted the Kitchen Shoals Beacon 30 minutes later and several minutes after that the faint outline of Bermuda as Ryan had predicted. The wind shifted as the sun rose and they trimmed sails and adjusted their course to the east when they got to Northeast Breakers Buoy and followed the edge of the barrier reef around its perimeter until they got to Kitchen Shoals Buoy, then turned in a westerly direction towards Town Cut and St. Georges. Ryan brought Clifton up on deck so he could relieve himself and Tory woke the children and the three of them joined Ryan on deck.

"Will you steer again? I want to call Bermuda Harbor Radio and shave before we get in. Otherwise immigration might not let us ashore. I should have called them 12 miles out and forgot."

"You're not that bad!" Then Tory looked more closely into his eyes and was suddenly very aware of the exhaustion that Ryan was finally allowing himself to feel. She reached out and ran the back of her hand across his beard stubble.

"And you're right, a shave is probably a good idea. After we get in and get organized I'll make sure you can sleep as long as you like."

"Will you put me to bed."

She smiled. "Yes, I'll tuck you in," and then added, "What's Bermuda Harbor Radio?"

"The Bermudans like anyone entering their waters to give them a heads up about 12 miles out. I sent them an email before we left with our details. They have a radar outpost on that tall hill up there and like everyone to check in with them before they enter the harbor."

"Oh," Tory answered, a little surprised.

St. George's harbor is a good one and the natural protection it affords vessels is immediate as you travel through the enlarged cut at its entrance. They reached the cut a half hour later and Ryan dropped and furled the sails before motoring through. The wind died and the seas calmed as they entered, and Tory, Jan and Willy were momentarily speechless as they took in the colors and textures so unique to Bermuda: turquoise blue water, pink sand and the gentle pastel colors of the stucco homes that were chalked tidily into the hillsides. Every one with a clean white painted roof to catch rainfall. Clifton's nose began twitching as his starved olfactory system drank in the scents and smells of the tropical island.

Jan knelt next to him and petted his head. She was the first to speak. "Mom, it's so soft and beautiful, its like nothing I've ever seen. Is it real?"

"I don't know honey. Ryan why didn't tell us it would be like this. It's incredible!"

"I thought I'd surprise you. I was afraid if I told you too much it would take away from your first impression. It is special though, isn't it?" All three nodded.

They came out the other side of the 'cut' and continued across the harbor towards the customs dock. Willy was the first to notice that virtually everyone on shore were driving motorcycles.

"Look mom, motorcycles!"

"That's another thing unique about this place," Ryan explained. "In an effort to keep congestion and pollution down, each household on the island is only allowed one car and almost everyone drives a moped, even elderly people. You can't even rent a car on the island."

"How will we get around then Ryan?" Jan asked.

"Well, I usually rent a moped. If it's alright with your mother we'll rent two of them and you and Willy can ride on the back."

Neither had ever ridden a motorcycle and exchanged excited looks before turning as one to Tory. "Can we Mom, please?"

Tory thought for a moment. "I don't know, I've never ridden one before. What do you think Ryan, can I learn to ride one of those well enough to avoid killing one of the kids or myself?"

"You just sailed a 42-boat halfway across the Atlantic. I wouldn't think a little old moped would be much of a challenge."

"Well, when you put it that way …," Tory assented.

They were approaching the customs dock as they finished the moped conversation. Ryan put the boat into neutral and told Tory to stand by the helm as he went below to contact customs and immigration on the radio. "Bermuda Customs, this is sailing vessel Parthenia, over."

The customs officer on duty immediately came back over the radio. "This is Bermuda Customs. Welcome back Mr. Cunningham. How may we help you today?"

Tory was impressed as she listened to the conversation through the companionway hatch and raised her eyebrows at Ryan as she listened to their exchange.

"Thank you for the kind salutation, it's good to be back. We're currently off your dock here in St. George's and would like to clear in with you, over."

"Understood sir, please raft alongside the Swan 65 at the dock and we'll be with you presently. "Are all your passengers U.S. citizens, over?"

"Affirmative."

"Jolly good. One of our men will be with you after you tie up."

"Thank you, Bermuda Customs, Parthenia standing by on 16."

Tory raised her eyebrows again as Ryan came back on deck. "Mr. Cunningham? I'm impressed. How come they know you so well?"

"I've been through here 15 or 20 times over the years although I can't say I've ever done anything to distinguish myself. I think a lot of it's just a lingering respect for mariners who arrive by sea."

Tory had noticed the accent of the customs officer. "Jolly good. Was that *chap* serious Ryan? I mean does everyone really talk with such a British accent here?"

"Yup. They speak the King's English here. Sounds strange, doesn't it?"

Ryan and Jan fished out the dock lines and the fenders from the lazaret as Tory held the boat a prudent distance off the dock and once they had them in place Ryan took the helm and eased Parthenia alongside the Swan 65. No one was aboard the other vessel to take their lines so he had Tory jump onto the other boat and Jan passed them to her. As they tied off, Clifton spotted another dog and barked a greeting.

"Boy mom, I know I'm looking forward to going ashore, but think how bad Clifton must want to go!" Jan remarked.

"I'm afraid that won't be possible Miss, unless you're arriving from the U.K. or another one of our possessions."

They all looked up onto the pier simultaneously at the source of the voice. It was a large black man in the blue uniform of Royal Bermuda Customs.

He then addressed himself to Ryan, "Terribly sorry Mr. Cunningham, but if you're arriving from the U.S., as I suspect, then your dog will either have to remain aboard for the duration of your stay or be impounded at one of our local veterinarians for a mandatory six month quarantine. Unfortunately, we have the same laws regarding the importation of pets as the U.K."

Ryan turned to his crew who had all remained silent to this point. "Well, you all heard the man. Clifton is not allowed ashore, so we'll all have to make a special effort to keep him company while we're here."

"Do you have any drugs or guns on board with you?"

Like most people, Willy, Jan, and Tory all immediately became nervous at this direct question, and although none of them did have anything illicit in their possession Ryan was immediately glad that he'd kept quiet about the weapons he'd hidden as he doubted any of them would have been able to lie convincingly. Ryan (as captain) answered for all of them. "No sir, with the exception of some prescription drugs in our medicine chest."

"Could we go below and inventory those please Mr. Cunningham, and at the same time we can fill out all the forms and review your passports."

Ryan replied in the affirmative and led the Customs officer below to the salon table. While Ryan worked below with the customs officer Tory, Jan, and Willy took Clifton forward on deck so they could talk out of range of the officer below.

"Mom, that man talks funny," Willy remarked.

"I know, that's called a British accent. I guess all the people here on the island talk that way," Tory responded.

Ryan completed the paperwork and drug inventory several minutes later and the customs officer returned to the dock after wishing them all a pleasant stay.

"That's too bad about Clifton. How are we going to keep him from swimming ashore? I know he'll try if he sees us heading off the boat," Tory said.

"Well, I've been thinking about that and the only way I can figure is for us to get a mooring or anchor out in the harbor, and whenever we do leave the boat we'll have to tie him on deck. He'll moan about it, but it's only for a few days. He'll live."

Through with customs, they slipped their lines and headed back down the harbor till they got to the Dinghy Club. Ryan picked up a club mooring and after inflating the Zodiac and tying an upset Clifton to a short lead on the foredeck, they all headed ashore for a hot shower and some local food. They walked into St. George's proper and had burgers and fries at the White Horse Tavern. After paying the check they walked out into St. George's square pausing at the old cedar stockades where hundreds of years ago criminals, witches, and blasphemers had been publicly pilloried and ridiculed for their supposed crimes. They lingered long enough for the children to pose with their necks and wrists stuck through the remedial medieval contraptions before moving onto the outdoor bike rental shop.

"And how may I help you all today sir?" inquired the elderly black shop owner.

"Well, we'd like two motorbikes big enough to carry the children and a few groceries, but easy to operate as the "Mrs." here (and Ryan slipped his arm over Tory's shoulder) has never ridden one and is a little nervous about the whole thing."

Jan giggled behind her hand as Tory rubbed her head on Ryan's shoulder playing the sweet, young wife. As he spoke Ryan moved over a few feet and pointed to two matching red Hondas that looked slightly futuristic in their styling.

"A good choice, sir. They're electric start, automatic, two-seaters and both have baskets on the rear for stowing groceries."

Jan and Willy looked at them with wide eyes. "Mom, these are awesome. Can we get them?" Jan asked.

Tory shrugged a "yes, deferring to Ryan's suggestion, and after showing the shop owner their licenses and filling out the requisite forms the owner went over the operation of the scooters and then had both of them ride around the square several times to get a feel for the brakes and throttle.

"Enjoy yourselves and remember to stay to the left," shouted the bike shop owner as they pulled out of the parking lot.

"What'd he mean, 'keep to the left' Ryan?" Tory asked.

"Sorry, I forgot to mention that. They drive on the other side of the road here."

Ryan pulled out first with Willy behind him on the seat. Tory hesitated momentarily. "It's cool Mom, you can do it. Just don't let them get away!" replied Jan excitedly.

Tory quickly looked off to her side, twisted the throttle grip and after a wobble or two was in hot pursuit with Jan egging her on from behind.

Rip Converse

(Ryan

(UTC)

Chapter 7

Geographically and climatically Bermuda is a tropical paradise, but seldom the ultimate destination of sailors. British influence is still strong on the small island and although the majority of the population wear shorts nine months of the year, these shorts are long in length, laundered and pressed with a stiff crease designed to reassure the wearers that despite the tropical climate and relaxed nature of the visitors that go there to vacation, order is being maintained. They also strictly enforce a policy of not allowing transients to disembark on their pristine little rock unless they have cash in their pocket, and some sort of conveyance off the island, be that a return plane ticket or a floating boat. This allows them to deport indigents, nonconformists, anarchists and people with bad table manners at the blink of an eye. As many of the sailors that travel the world oceans have little money and a decidedly relaxed outlook on nearly everything, most of them move on after short stays to replenish their depleted stores.

Despite the relatively uptight nature of the natives (compared with their Caribbean cousins) Tory and Ryan were not indigent nor did they have any interest in overthrowing the government. As a result, they were welcome. For the first time in their lives, neither had to be anywhere at any specific time nor had to live up to another's expectations. Bermuda quickly became a very special place for them, especially considering their difficult passage, and they decided to go with the flow and spend several weeks enjoying the island and themselves rather than moving on after a quick replenishment of their supplies as originally planned.

After three days moored in front of the Dinghy Club, two old friends of Ryan's offered them a mooring in front of their house across the harbor. Ryan had first met Mike and Jill some 15 years earlier after tearing his mainsail in a storm in one of the first Marion-Bermuda races. They were the local sailmakers and over the ensuing years the three of them had established a close reciprocal relationship.

They frequently stayed with Ryan when they traveled to the U.S., and vice versa. The friendship was a comfortable one and Mike and Jill were pleased to offer them the use of their mooring and the kitchen and hot showers in their house. Further adding to the convenience of the situation for Ryan and Tory were Mike and Jill's three children ranging in age from five to 10 who quickly made friends with Jan and Willy. The five children were content for hours at a time in their own company hunting salamanders, swimming in the turquoise waters and playing in the open fields behind the house. Despite the fact that Tory was doing a home study program with Jan and Willy, the parents took turns watching the large brood when they weren't in school or daycare and on special occasions they hired the next door neighbor to sit when they wanted to go out for an adults only meal in the evening. When Ryan and Tory wanted to go out to an AA meeting they simply left Willy and Jan with Mike and Jill.

"What are you thinking about?" Ryan asked. They were sitting side by side on the foredeck of Parthenia taking in the last remnants of the sun's light under a cloudless blue sky. They had changed out of their bathing suits earlier, Ryan into shorts and a long sleeved shirt, Tory into a short dungaree skirt and loose cotton blouse, and despite the added clothes, both were starting to feel the chill of the evening air heightened by the sunburn they'd acquired during the afternoon. The children were ashore at Mike and Jill's and camping behind their house with the other children. Clifton was asleep in the cockpit.

"I don't really know. I guess I'm healing and don't know whether to laugh or cry half the time. On one hand I feel very sad about the pain and heartache I caused everyone in recent years. On the other, I feel healthier as a human being than I have in my whole life. As if I might be able make everything right again, whatever that means."

Ryan put one arm around her shoulders and reached across her lap taking one of her hands in his.

"The healing takes a long time. You spent years walking into the woods, so don't expect to walk out in just a few days."

She leaned in closer and rested her head on his shoulder. "I know, I've heard that expression before. It's just that I'm impatient and want to make everything right again, *now*; not years from now."

"I think you're doing a great job. Have you noticed the change in Jan in the last few weeks? She actually smiles and laughs now. I think that's incredible progress."

A single tear rolled down Tory's face and she smiled, reached up and gently pulled Ryan's head in towards hers. "Ryan, I owe you a lot."

"No, you don't owe me any ..."

"Let me finish. I'm trying to say thank you. Thanks for giving me the space to grow and work through all this without making me feel pressured or obligated. You've given me the freedom to work through all of this without any preconditions or expectations. It's one of the first times in my life that I haven't felt pressured to do or be a certain way in order to win someone else's approval. I'm grateful to you for that." Tory tilted his head down to hers and kissed him; tentatively at first, and then with all the warmth and feeling that she was feeling at that moment.

Ryan held back at first, then relaxed, allowing himself to fall into her teary warmth. Her lips were warm, full and wet and her gentle kiss quickly became insistent, almost desperate. He pulled back, knowing that if they went any further their relationship would be forever altered.

"Tory, wait. We should discuss this. Are we really ready...?"

"Oh Ryan, I don't know anything for certain, but it sure feels right. May I suggest that you please shut up and make love to me, and stop rambling?"

"Rambling? This is a pretty heavy decision we're about to make. Don't you think that we should discuss it a little?"

"We've already discussed it a hundred times. Every time either one of us looks at the other we have a conversation in our head. I know you and trust you and I'm not exactly making this decision on the spur of the moment. I'm not asking you for a commitment, nor do I know if I have the wherewithal yet to make a decent partner to someone else but I haven't been with anyone in almost a year and a half and I really want you."

Ryan's feelings were similar to Tory's insofar that he did trust her and heaven knew that he'd wanted her from the first day they met, but they were going into territory that frightened him, because he felt so strongly. Normally he was able to maintain an emotional distance from his partners and that was no longer the case with her. He was scared to want anyone so much.

Tory sensed his continuing hesitation and slid her hand along the inside of his thigh and up the hem of his loose shorts gently stroking him and ending further verbal discourse. He moaned with pleasure and embraced her.

"No, just stay where you are." Tory straddled his lap and slowly unbuttoned the buttons on his shirt, peeled back both sides, and ran her fingers over his chest and then down the muscled sides of his abdomen, her touch alternately strong like a masseuse and then whisper-like with just the tips of her nails and he lay there for several minutes trying to store away the sensations of her first touch and unashamed desire for him. After a while he opened his eyes and shifted his focus to the small, hard, breasts only inches from his face, and reached out and traced one finger down the center of her chest. She tossed her head back, stretching the thin cotton weave of her top across her nipples and let out a groan of her own as he ran his palms over her breasts and traced the undersides with his thumbs.

She leaned down and kissed him again. "You have no idea how good that feels."

"I might."

He moved both hands to her sides and then slid them up her rib cage gathering the blouse as he went, revealing first her taught belly, then rib cage and finally two flawless, upturned breasts. Her nipples were so hard that the blouse caught on them as he raised it past them.

"You are..." he struggled to find the word. "Perfect," he finally finished.

"That's the best you can do?" Tory giggled and slapped at his chest playfully. She shifted her position backwards some and gathered his erection through the material of his shorts with one hand.

It was Ryan's turn to laugh. "That, is a testament to how hot I find you."

Tory straddled his stomach, reached behind her back and slid his shorts over his hips and then pulled them off maintaining eye contact the whole time. As she did, her dungaree skirt slid the rest of the way up her thighs revealing a tiny, white, silk G-string that was failing miserably in its implied warranty to contain and provide coverage for the swollen mound beneath. The thin silk was wet and tightly stretched over her outer lips. Ryan slid two fingers underneath the edge of the tight, wet, material and rubbed one of his thumbs over her small bud. Tory responded by lowering herself onto the erection that lay hard against his belly and gently slid her silk clad mound over the length of his cock. Ryan was so sensitized from his two-month abstinence that he could feel the texture of the silk in spite of the warm, viscous juices that soaked it and groaned again, reaching without thinking to her hips so that he could slide her back and forth along his length. She reached down, pulled the crotch of her panties aside, lowered herself again, and continued to slide her wet lips up and down the length of Ryan's cock, leaning slightly forward so that her clitoris made more direct contact.

Neither had much staying power and Ryan was losing the small measure of control he'd exercised to this point. The feeling of her erect clitoris sliding against him was heightened and exaggerated by the cool evening breeze that blew over their genitals. He grabbed her even more firmly by the hips and simultaneously pulled her down, and back and forth along his length with increasing speed and force as the pressure built within him. Tory was herself starting to lose all control and reached between her legs, spread her lips further and shifted her angle again.

"Don't stop Ryan, whatever you do, don't stop," she cried out between clenched teeth. Stopping was the last thing on Ryan's mind and instead he raised his ass off the deck of the boat and pulled her down with more force, at the same time craning his head up and forward to take one of her nipples into his mouth. It was as if every nerve ending in her body was direct wired to that nipple and as he took it between his teeth Tory started to orgasm, in great heaves and jerks. Her orgasm acted like a trigger on Ryan, sending him over the edge and he cried out in a guttural, almost primal way as he exploded with two months of pent up desire. Tory slowed eventually and in long, gentler strokes up and down his length, milked every possible drop of semen from him. She fell forward onto his chest, embraced him, and rubbed herself against his wetness.

They lay there in the moments that followed glowing, their hearts pounding and echoing to each other in the now still night without moving for several minutes and then started the slow but inevitable ascent back to the real world. Ryan reached up and gently brushed the hair from her face and she lowered her lips to his and kissed him tenderly.

"Are you OK?" he asked after several moments. When he'd brushed her hair back he'd felt the cool wetness of tears on her cheek.

"I am very OK. That was wonderful."

"Why the tears?"

"It's a woman thing. You know, sometimes we laugh when we're sad, other times we cry when we're happy. It makes perfect sense to me." They moved below onto the big bunk in the main salon.

They continued off and on all night with the energy and determination of long-distance runners. It was as if every lover each had had in the past was in preparation for this one grueling night where the passions of each fought ceaselessly to better the others'. There were no rules and they descended to the crudity and bullish power of street fighters several times. Most of the time, however, their battle was fought with the finesse and smoothness of prizefighters. At about 4 a.m. they declared a truce.

"Tory, I can't go on, I'm absolutely raw. As it is I'm going to need several days of bedrest before I'll be able to move again."

"You. What about me? Now I know how the Sabine women felt."

Ryan glanced at his watch. "It's 4:15. Let's try and get a little sleep before the horde of urchins descends on us. They'll be back in another three hours."

Tory groaned and swung her legs off the bunk. "Okay, but this place looks like there was an orgy in here," and tilted her head towards a half full bottle of olive oil on the table next to them. The exterior was an oily mess and what contents weren't in or around the bottle seemed to be covering them both.

"I don't know where you got the idea for using that, but I expect for the rest of my life every time I pick up an olive oil bottle to make salad dressing or sauté I'm going to have a big smile on my face and blush. I, for one, have to take a shower and we really should clean up the cabin some before the kids get back."

"Ok. You take your shower and I'll pick up," Ryan replied.

Ryan cleaned up the small cabin as Tory showered and then made up the bunk with fresh sheets.

Tory emerged from the beautification chamber. "Your turn."

"Thanks, I'll be right out."

By the time Ryan finished Tory was half asleep in the freshly made bed. He slid between the cool sheets next to her, spooned along the length of her body and she fell soundly asleep. Ryan lay there conscious for a few moments longer absorbing the smell of her washed hair, the feel of her body and the small upturned breast in his hand and quickly followed her into a deep, contented sleep.

Their earlier jest about being descended on by a horde of urchins was not far off the mark and three hours later all five children pulled alongside giggling at each other. Jan and Willy were sitting side by side attempting to row Mile and Jill's rowboat in unison. Due to their disparate size and level of rowing skills the other three were in hysterics by the time they finally rowed the short distance out to Parthenia from shore. Willy had fallen backwards off his seat several times, failing to catch a good purchase on the water with his oar but adamantly refused to let one of the older children row.

"Hey Mom. Check this out. The shrimp is rowing," Jan cried out to Parthenia.

"I'm not a shrimp and I can row as well as you," he retorted.

"In your dreams Willy." One of the others shouted and the other four broke out in fresh hysterics. Clifton, happy to have company, was at the rail with his tail wagging, adding to the general melee by moaning and barking. Despite all the noise it was not until they crashed into the side of the boat that Ryan and Tory finally stirred.

"There's a whole boatload of reality boarding us. Are you ready?" Ryan asked.

"Oh God, what was I thinking when I decided to have children?" Tory replied. "Let me up. I want to put on some clothes before they all pile into the cabin. You better put on a pair of shorts, too. And while you're at it, restrain that thing. Christ, is it always so hard?"

119

Ryan laughed. "Around you. Maybe I should go and slam it in a hatch or something."

"Well, trouser it, at least. I don't want to scare the children. Tory departed with a smile and stumbled across the cabin and into the toilet just as Willy stuck his head down into the cabin.

"Hey, Ryan. How come you're still asleep? Is Mom here?"

"Hi sport. Yeah, she's in the head and will be out in a second. Why don't you guys take Clifton up on the foredeck and role the ball with him or something while I get up."

"OK."

Jan stuck her head in the hatch alongside Willy's. "God, you guys are still asleep."

"Christ, there must be a million kids up there," Ryan mumbled to himself, then gathered the sheet around his midsection and pausing briefly to look at his tired image in the cabin mirror, stumbled into the forward cabin to change in privacy.

They'd promised to take all the kids to a stone grotto called Devils Hole that day and after feeding Clifton and tying him on the foredeck they all rowed ashore making two round trips in the dinghy, due to their large numbers.

Devils Hole is a naturally formed cavern on the shore of Harrington Sound on the northeast end of the island. It's connected to the ocean by a small subterranean passage. What attracts children and adults alike is the large number of fish and turtles that were trapped in there years ago, that have continued to thrive and breed, surviving off one another. The opening to the ocean is large enough to allow the tides in and out (effectively changing the water daily), but not so large that the bigger fish inside can escape. Built around its internal perimeter are catwalks that allow visitors to look down on the fish in the cavern. For a modest sum, management provides visitors with lines and fresh bait to fish for these trapped animals. The catch is, nothing is ever caught as there are no hooks on the ends of the lines. But in the fertile minds of children there is always the chance that he or she *might* catch something, and this tends to keep the kids coming back time and again. They all crowded the railing to see who could bring the biggest fish to the surface. Ryan and Tory hung back some in the relative darkness on the catwalk and alternately held hands and stole occasional kisses. Both were exhausted from their amorous marathon, but enough magic remained from the night before to keep them awake and sensitive to each other's space.

"How're you doing this morning?" he asked.

Tory leaned into him and put her head on his shoulder. "I haven't felt this good in a long time."

"Me either."

"Think we made a mistake?" she asked.

"Nope. What's next?" he replied.

"I haven't a clue. I guess we just go with it."

And they did just that for the next few days, stealing as much time as possible alone to talk, make love and celebrate their expanded relationship. For Ryan it was the first time in many years that he felt comfortable receiving and sharing affection. Giving affection had never been a problem and he was in fact quite practiced at that, but past partners had always reached a point where they sensed that it was a one-way street and they ultimately formed resentments and became frustrated at his inability to share himself. In reality Ryan had a very poor self-image and didn't really believe in his ability to be there for anyone else. A lot of it was due to his own years of alcoholism and drug use and the lingering feeling that he was "less than" other men and undependable. And why should he take the risk involved in becoming soul mates with another? He'd learned as a teenager, with the death of his father, that it's dangerous to invest too much love in another human being. You might wake up one morning and find them gone.

Tory wasn't much different in that she also had a very poor self-image and perhaps that was why things were working for them. Two hearts that had grown hard and dark in protective isolation began to open in the presence of each other.

"I'm envious. Things seem very special between you and Tory," Mike remarked the next day. "I don't think I've ever seen you so close to someone else in all the years that I've known you, and with kids besides!"

Ryan and Mike were in Mike's loft re-cutting Parthenia's working jib. Ryan thought for a moment before replying. "They are special, and you know it's funny, kids always bored the shit out of me. But it seems to be different with them. I actually like these two as people! I could never understand how people like you and Jill could put up with kids but they're wonderful. Sure, they're selfish and immature at times, but it feels good to be needed and wanted."

"Well, you do lose a lot of freedom, but Jill and I never regretted our decision. Hey, have you guys decided when you're going to head out?"

"We were thinking of staying another four or five days. Does that work for you?"

"Stay as long as you like. It's been nice having you around."

Later that evening both families were crowded around Mike and Jill's TV after dinner when the phone rang. Jill answered and came back into the room after a few moments.

"Tory, it's for you, some older woman."

Tory briefly exchanged glances with Ryan and walked into the other room. Ryan couldn't hear the conversation and wondered who would be calling and why. Tory's grandparents and her two friends in Sippican were the only ones with their number in Bermuda. After a few minutes Ryan got up and went into the kitchen just as Tory was hanging up the phone. She looked shaken and turned into Ryan's arms and put her head on his shoulder.

"What's happened?"

"That was my grandmother. My grandfather had a stroke and they don't think he's going to make it."

"I'm sorry, I know you care a lot about him. What do you want to do?" Ryan replied.

"I told her that I'd fly back tomorrow. She has to make some difficult decisions over the next few days and could really use some support. I guess there's little, if any, brain function and the doctors think he should be taken off life support. She doesn't know what to do. Wasn't it just yesterday I was thinking that things were going along a little too smoothly, and wham! Something like this happens. Does it ever get easy?"

122

Ryan stroked her back as he thought for a minute. "No, I guess not, it's just life. Maybe we get a little better dealing with stuff, but it still happens. Focus on how special he was to you and be grateful that he was a part of your life."

"I know, you're right."

"Didn't you say your grandfather was the only person in your family who really stood behind you and never gave up on you over the last few years?"

Tory nodded.

"Do you have any idea how much it must have meant to him to see you get sober and recover your life? You must have made him very happy."

"I guess, but my heart still hurts. Will you wait around for me for a few days?"

"Of course. Take as long as you need. It's not like I have some special rendezvous I have to be at. I've got plenty of little projects on the boat to keep me busy while you're away. Would it be easier if I watched the kids here while you're gone?"

"I hadn't thought of that. Let me talk it over with them."

"Whatever you decide is fine with me."

"Thanks."

Tory told the children what was going on and after thinking it through decided that it was better if she went on her own. She didn't expect to be gone for more than a week and figured that she could probably be more available to her grandmother if she went alone.

Rip Converse

Chapter 8

She left early the next morning on the first flight out, with a scheduled stop in New York before continuing to Boston. As luck would have it she was greeted by the first major snowstorm of the winter and it wasn't until almost 7 p.m. that her flight finally arrived at Logan Airport. She'd told her grandmother not to worry about transportation for her and rented a car and drove the 90 miles to her grandparent's small town in western Massachusetts. She finally arrived at about 10 p.m., exhausted from the long day of travel through the remnants of the blizzard. Rather than going immediately to her grandmother's she instead went directly to the hospital.

The local hospital was a small one and generally used by the residents of the town for emergencies and minor surgical procedures with most preferring to go into Boston for anything major. It was this "small town" attitude that enabled her to get permission from the night charge nurse to see her grandfather at such a late hour. After a brief stop in the ladies' room to put herself together, she continued down the quiet corridor to his door.

Tory entered quietly not knowing what to expect and was surprised to find a woman giving him a sponge bath and reading softly from a bible that was propped up next to his head. Except for a reading light that was turned on at the head of the bed, the room was dark and peaceful.

"I'm sorry, I didn't know there was anyone in here with him. Am I interrupting?"

The woman who turned at the sound of Tory's voice was in her mid-40s, on the heavy side, with soft, blonde curls that surrounded her face in an almost cherubic fashion.

"Oh hello, you must be Tory, the granddaughter," the woman said in a matter of fact way. "Your grandmother said you'd be arriving today or tomorrow."

"I flew in from Bermuda today and wanted to see Pop before going to my grandmother's. How is he?"

"Well, I think he's doing pretty well. It was a little nip and tuck the first day, but I think he's stabilized and gaining strength."

Tory was confused. "Oh, I was under the impression that he'd had a pretty massive stroke and had lost all brain funct..."

The woman put a finger to her lips indicating that Tory should stop what she was saying.

"Well yes, as I said he did have a tough time of it last night but I think things are looking up, and with the good lord to help us through I expect the very best for your grandfather."

"Are you a nurse?"

"No dear. I guess you would call me a nurse's aide, but in my case, in addition to making patients a little more comfortable, I attend to their spiritual needs. Give me a hand for a second, would you? I want to turn him back over so that I can give him a shave."

Tory hesitated for a second as she looked down on the frail figure of her grandfather. His skin was almost translucent and seemed to hang off his limbs, emphasizing his vulnerability. He'd been a physically powerful man and it was immediately clear to Tory that the vitality she associated with him, was gone.

"He doesn't look..." Again, Tory was cut off by the woman's finger on her lips.

"You turn the legs as I turn the top half, and mind that IV, it took them quite some time to find a good vein and we don't want them sticking him full of holes again."

Tory did as instructed and they were able to turn him in one smooth motion. After adjusting the pillows beneath his head so that he was propped up, Myrna pulled the sheet up to the top of his chest then sent Tory into the adjoining bathroom to fetch a pan of warm water.

Tory carefully shuffled back across the room several minutes later trying not to spill any. "Here you are being so kind to Pop and I don't even know your name."

"It's Myrna, and it's my pleasure. I spend a lot of time with sick folks and have a real good feel for people. I can tell from your grandfather's aura that he's a kind and good man. I'm sure he would do the same for me if our situations were reversed."

Tory was a bit put off by her choice of words. Myrna sounded more spiritual than practical. "Well, I just want you to know it's appreciated."

"Thank you. But as I said before, it's my pleasure. That's what the good lord put me on this earth for and I try to do my best."

For the next 15 minutes Tory watched in silence as Myrna carefully shaved him and then brushed his hair. After completing her tasks Tory looked down on her grandfather and although she knew the man before her was no longer a part of her world, she had to admit he looked more at peace. Myrna also looked down on her work and after carefully patting a last lock of hair into place, leaned back in her chair with a satisfied look on her face and said, "That's better. I know appearance was important to him and he should rest more comfortably now."

Tory knew she was right and inwardly made one of those life connections; that although Pop was old by her standards, and a "grandfather" in her mind, on a different level, he'd forever been a young man in his own mind and cared very much about the face he presented to the rest of the world. As Tory thought further on the subject she realized that her grandfather had in fact been quite a ladies man in his day and was thought of as quite charming by most of the women that he'd come in contact with over the years. He'd simply gotten older without really taking note of that fact. In his mind he was probably still the rake that he'd been 30 or 40 years before. "How strange," she thought and wondered if she too would wake up one morning years later in a hospital bed and suddenly realize that it was all over, that her life had passed before her and was suddenly at an end. Or even worse, what if it all ended with the speed of her grandfather's stroke, without time for appropriate reflection.

"Tory, I have to leave now and look in on some of my other friends. Will you be OK?"

Tory looked up misty eyed. "Oh, I think so. We have a lot of memories to go over together." She reached out and took Myrna's hand in hers. "Thank you for being here."

After Myrna left, Tory sat with her grandfather's hand in hers. She knew that the man she'd loved was gone, but the heart that had loved her unconditionally for so many years continued to pump warm blood through the hand she held in her own. She found it difficult to reconcile one with the other. Myrna had stopped her from speaking earlier whenever her comments turned to her grandfather's condition on the chance that he was still able to hear the conversations around him, despite his coma. Alone with him, she knew her grandfather would never hear or understand earthly conversations again. That man was gone, never to return, and as she tried to remember and impress into her memory everything she'd loved about him; his bear hugs that had made everything better as a child, the feel and sound of his whiskers on her face, his big, rough hands that seemed to swallow hers when they walked, smiles, words of praise and support when all others around her had given up, the way he split logs and poked a fire, read aloud, pet his Golden Retriever, and sailed his boat. She smiled at her memory of his love of buttery, corn-on-the-cob. Sometimes he would eat a dozen ears if it was fresh enough. She reached out to touch his forehead one last time, brushed a kiss against his still warm cheek, thanked him for being a part of her life, and turned to leave the room. When she reached the door she stopped, feeling as though something had been forgotten or left unsaid and walked back to the bedside, knelt beside it, and gathered one of his hands in her own again.

"Pops, I know you're gone, and I don't know if you can hear me, but if you could just somehow give me some of your strength to stay sober and be the person...?" She didn't really know what she was asking, but before she could finish the sentence a warm energy seemed to suffuse and fill the space above her. It built until it was almost crackling in its intensity. This energy hovered above her gathering strength and organizing itself, transformed itself into a brilliant white light, and then fell on Tory like a waterfall, washing over and into her head, neck and shoulders. The hair on her neck and arms stood on end in response and her whole body rushed as if she'd taken amphetamines or heard a perfect harmony. Simultaneously, she was filled with feelings of strength, peace and confidence.

She continued to kneel for several minutes, unsure of what had just taken place and too dizzy to risk standing. When she did finally arise, it was not with feelings of sadness, loss or anger at his passing. It was instead with a sense of completion and joy at having had him in her life for all the years that she had. She knew he was at peace and that his passing was as natural and right as his full life had been.

"Thank you," she whispered. "And don't worry about Grams. I'll help her get through this." She placed the hand that she'd been holding gently on his chest, turned, and walked quietly from the room.

As she drove the short distance from the hospital to her grandmother's, Tory tried to collect herself and prepare for the reunion. She hoped she would be able to make good on her final promise to Pops. She and he may have shared their goodbyes, but the same was probably not true for her grandmother. Grams was 'old world' and her very life and purpose had centered around Pops. Whereas many have time to prepare for the loss of a spouse through protracted illness, Pops' stroke had been sudden and unexpected. Adding to her anxiety was the fact that Tory had never been particularly close to her grandmother. With the exception of the phone call in Bermuda, the last time they'd spoken was 16 months ago when they'd discovered that Tory had been stealing from them to support her habit. As a result, Grams had forbidden her entry to their home and although she'd continued to maintain contact with Pops during her period in the treatment center and throughout her stay at the halfway house, Grams had wanted nothing to do with her.

Tory recalled the day she'd last seen her grandmother. She'd found out that her grandparents were intending to drive into Boston for the day, and after parking down the street and waiting for them to leave she let herself into their house through a side window. Her intention had been to pretty much clean them out, making it look like a house burglary. Until then her thievery had been limited to stealing money out of their wallets when she visited, and on one occasion a gold chain out of her grandmother's jewelry box. On that fated day she'd worked quite diligently for about 15 minutes disconnecting the TVs, VCR and stereo and had then stacked all the electronics and several other items of value including her grandmother's jewelry box and family silver near the breezeway door so that she could easily load it into the trunk of her car. Before leaving she'd decided to have a few drinks out of their liquor cabinet. She ended up having more than a few, passed out on their living room couch and awakened to the panicked voice of her grandfather.

"Tory, Tory, are you alright?" he'd asked.

Not immediately sure of where she was, Tory had opened her eyes and looked up into his. "I don't know ... where am I?" she replied trying to shake off her fog.

Initially he'd been unable to wake her and Grams had hurried to the kitchen to call 911. While in there dialing she'd noticed all the items that Tory had planned on stealing and hung up before getting an answer. She returned to the living room.

"George, she's not sick, she's just high again. She's gone too far this time and I think we should call the police. Money out of our wallets was one thing, but you should see the stack of stuff next to the back door. She was going to steal all my jewelry and my mother's silver."

"No Virginia, wait. She's sick! Can't you see she needs our help?" he'd replied.

Normally Tory would have tried to lie her way out of things and made up some story about how she'd interrupted the burglars and had in fact saved all of their possessions, but she was tired of the lies at this point and answered her grandfather's questions as honestly as she could.

"Tory, what is it you're taking that would make you steal from your family?"

"It's bad Pops, real bad. I snort cocaine, I smoke crack, and I drink. All the time. I never sleep more than a couple of hours because I need it. Please try and understand, I *need* it, not just want it. I have to have it. The real me would never steal from you and Grams, but the person you're talking to right now would, and has. I'm so sorry but I don't know what else to do!"

"George, I still think we ought to call the police. We don't know anything about this stuff she puts in her body. They can probably get her some help."

"No. She's not a criminal, she's sick!" he'd snapped back. He paced back and forth in front of the couch for several minutes before speaking again.

"Tory, your grandmother is right, we don't know anything about these things that you put into your body. I do know that I love you though and I believe you can pull yourself back together if we can get you some help. If we can, will you take it?"

Tory was crying at this point and felt as though she was going to die from shame. Pops had indicated that he still loved and believed in her and these sentiments meant a great deal. At that moment she felt so much guilt and was so tired of the charade she'd been living she would have killed herself if he'd asked.

"Pops, I'll do anything you ask. I'm so tired of living this way."

"Do *you* want help? I'm not asking you to do this for me. I'm asking if you'll do it for yourself?"

"Yes Pops, anything, I'll do anything to end this."

Her recovery began at that moment and within 24 hours she was checked into a 30-day, residential treatment program. Throughout her stay he'd driven the 120 miles each way every weekend to support her. Grams wanted nothing to do with her and didn't believe she could recover. She'd taken everything very personally and still to this day looked on Tory as a person with weak moral character rather than as a sick person. On one level Tory resented this, on another she took it as a personal challenge of sorts that she might someday be able to demonstrate to her grandmother that she was a good person worthy of her trust again. With these thoughts and memories running through her mind she quietly knocked on Grams' door and then let herself in, afraid to wake her if she was asleep.

The house was quiet and dark with the exception of a single light in the living room. Tory took off her coat and softly called out her grandmother's name not wanting to startle her if she was awake. After hanging her coat in the hall closet, she walked into the living room. Her grandmother was there, where she'd obviously been napping while awaiting Tory's arrival and was slowly swinging her legs off the couch and out from underneath a mohair blanket as Tory walked in.

"Don't get up Grams," Tory said and sat down beside her on the couch. "How are you doing?"

"Hi dear. I guess I'm doing all right. How are you? You're the one who just did all the traveling."

"I'm tired, but I haven't been traveling the whole time. I stopped by the hospital on the way to look in on Pops. He seems to be resting comfortably."

"Yes, I guess he is. From what the doctors say he's in great shape physically and could literally go on for years. He has a very strong heart you know."

"Yes, and a good one besides," Tory replied. An awkward silence followed.

Grams gave in first and filled the void with a detailed description of how it had happened and how good all the neighbors had been, but she seemed to carefully avoid touching on either of the two subjects that both knew must be discussed. Tory took the lead.

"I know this is probably difficult for you to discuss but have the doctors discussed with you how much damage was done to his brain?"

Her grandmother kneaded her hands together for a few moments before answering. When she did, she showed the first real emotion since Tory's arrival.

"I know I've been going on about how well things are going but the truth of the matter is I don't know what to do. Sure, his heart's beating away, and the doctors say he could live for years, but they all agree that he'll never wake up, well not really anyway. The test they do to measure brain activity shows an absolutely flat line and they say it's not something that can change or be reversed. Simply put, George is already gone and simply forgot to take himself with him! Oh God, it sounds as though I'm making a joke of the whole thing and I'm not. This is so unlike him to leave loose ends."

Tory knew she wasn't joking but smiled at her choice of words anyway because she knew her grandfather would be smiling if he were listening in. She put her arm around her grandmother's shoulders. "It's OK, Grams. I know you weren't joking but I'm smiling because I know he would be if he were here."

"Yes, I suppose he would," and tilted her head up towards the ceiling. "George, if you're listening, I want you to tell us just what in the hell we are supposed to do."

They both laughed and shared a hug. Grams turned back towards her.

"What should I do Tory? The doctors want me to think about disconnecting his life-support and I don't know as I can do that. I would feel like I was betraying our relationship and everything it stood for the last 49 years. It seems so fundamental. I mean we took care of each other for all those years in good times and bad. For me to be the one to make that decision seems so unfair. God's supposed to make decisions like that, not me!"

Tory thought hard for several moments before replying. She knew that her response at this point would not really have anything to do with what was best for her grandfather as in her mind, he was gone. Her grandmother, however, had the rest of her life before her and would have to live with herself and the decision she made for years to come.

"Grams, did you two ever discuss something like this happening?"

"Not really specifically. Your grandfather was kind of funny about the subject. It was almost as if it was a non-issue. I think he expected that someday we would both start to get old, *as if we aren't now*, and that eventually in some very predictable fashion our health would start to fail and we would move into one of those complexes that offers varying degrees of care in a community setting. It never really dawned on him that he already was old. I guess a lot of that was because he was never sick and still had all his hobbies and such. His life was a full one and there weren't any early warning signs like high blood pressure."

"Well, what about if he was disabled through an accident or something? Did it ever come up in that context?" Tory asked.

"He made off-hand comments about friends of ours who got sick and eventually died, like Bert Reiss, his old college buddy. Bert had a long fight with cancer and was in and out of the hospital for several years. I know that towards the end George would come back from the hospital and say things like he never wanted to go through something like that, but we both always assumed that there would be a transition period where we could discuss things and get used to the idea of one of us being gone. I know what you're asking me, and yes, George did say on more than one occasion that he wouldn't want a bunch of machines keeping him alive. But right now, that's not the case. It's almost as though he's sleeping. There are no machines attached to him and the only help he's getting is the food he gets through that IV line."

Tory paused again before saying anything. "No matter what happens Grams, I know you'll make the right decision. I know you love him very much. Let's get some sleep and talk more in the morning?"

Grams looked into her eyes for a long time before replying, "Tory, I'm sorry."

"About what?"

"I haven't been much of a grandmother to you over the last few years. George always believed in you but I'm ashamed to say, I didn't. You promised us so many times before that things would be different 'this time,' and they just never were. The next time we'd see you, you'd be high on something else or drunk again. I now know that I was wrong. Please forgive me for not having your grandfather's faith in you. I can tell things are somehow different inside you now. Before when we talked I always had this feeling in my stomach that you were trying to run something past me or manipulate me in some way, and for the first time in a long time I feel like I'm talking to the little girl I used to know. It's nice to have you back and I'm grateful to you for being here for your grandfather and me. I always loved you, I just didn't know what to do with you."

Grams' words meant more to Tory than she could ever know. They were her reacceptance into the only community of family she had.

"Grams, there's a lot I still feel like I have to apologize for, but for now I just want to say, 'Thank you.' I never stopped loving you either but felt powerless and frustrated every time I tried to live up to your expectations. Whenever I thought of the way I treated you and Pops over the last several years my heart hurt with shame. Between your forgiveness and my relationship with the man I'm sailing south with, I feel the beginnings of hope again. I still feel ashamed about the things I did in the past but with your forgiveness and love I might someday forgive myself. I love you both very much."

Grams listened, grateful for the return of the granddaughter she thought she'd lost. The two of them hugged and cried together for several moments.

"A fine pair we are," her grandmother finally said.

"I know. We'll talk more in the morning?"

During the next two days, two outside neurologists came in to examine Pops and gave opinions on his condition and the likelihood of recovery. Both agreed that his health was fine and that he would probably live for several years given proper care. They also agreed that there was no chance of any cognitive recovery due to the extent of the hemorrhaging. Quite simply, except for his autonomic functions, the mind and memories of Pops had died and disappeared forever with no likelihood that he would ever wake up. Both Tory and her grandmother knew this before they called in the outside specialists, but it was important to Grams to be absolutely sure. She knew he would've done the same for her and that she would never have another night's sleep if she didn't go through the motions.

The third day into Tory's stay Grams made the decision to withdraw the minimal life support that he'd been receiving, and after signing the necessary forms their family doctor of many years simply withdrew the thin tube that was Pops' sole source of nutrition and water. They sat quietly in Pops' room afterwards each steeped in her own private memories of the man who lay before them. There was little to say that hadn't been covered by the two of them over the last three days and although Tory would have supported any decision she made, Grams felt strongly that it should be her decision alone, and looked solemnly on it as the final and perhaps most important one of her lifelong journey with Pops. The doctor had indicated that it would take three to five days before dehydration completed the process that the stroke had begun, and that he would be in no pain as his system gradually slowed down until his electrolyte level became critical and his heart simply stopped. Grams never left his side during that time and took over the duties that the strange little woman had been performing the night Tory arrived. Each day she carefully bathed and shaved Pops and read out loud from the bible which was something that he'd done every morning of his adult life. She was under no illusions that the man she read and talked to during this period could hear her or understand her in any traditional sense, but on a different level, on one of the heart and soul, she sensed that George was lingering, not afraid of what was next for him, rather out of concern for her, that she would be able to go on and finish her life without him.

Tory stayed at her side throughout, in awe of the depth of Grams' love and commitment and wondered if she would ever be able to love another so completely that she could make that final decision, no matter how remote the prospect of recovery, that would forever remove that person from her life. To never look on their face again, every line and wrinkle a shared memory, to never hear their soft breath, peaceful and reassuring in bed next to you.

Pops finally passed at 2:30 in the morning of the fourth day with both Tory and Grams at his side. One moment there, the next gone; a lifetime of love, joy, hardship, work, commitment and creativity suddenly nothing but memories in the lives of the few people he'd touched in his time on earth. Grams and Tory cried quietly together at the finality of it all and after a last kiss to the still warm cheek of the man who had meant so much to her, Tory left the room so that her grandmother could say her final good-byes alone and stood in the hall feeling physically and emotionally drained from the four-day vigil.

She stayed on an additional four days through the memorial service and long enough to write a will and set up a trust fund for Jan and Willy. Her grandfather had left her a substantial sum of money. She didn't know when she'd next be back in the U.S. and figured it was as good enough a time as any to start acting responsible with her inheritance. During her stay with Grams she'd spoken with Ryan and the children almost daily on the phone and not knowing how long her grandmother would be of this world had asked Ryan if he would consider being a fiduciary trustee for the children's trust. Ryan agreed with only a moment's thought.

There was a long tearful goodbye with her grandmother and a commitment on both of their parts to stay in close touch, before she left for the airport and her return flight to Bermuda. Pleased that she'd been able to mend things and regain the trust of her Grandmother, she also knew that they'd never share the same close relationship that she'd shared with Pops. His love for her had been blind and unconditional and she knew she'd have to live many years before encountering anything like it again. For the first time since her arrival she was alone in her own head and silently mourned her loss, unaware of everything else as she traveled back to Ryan and the children.

Rip Converse

Chapter 9

At 9 a.m. White Lady cleared the Kitchen Shoals buoy. Edward had the crew make final preparations for their landfall in Bermuda. Even though they'd cleaned and washed down the engine room after loading the cocaine in the Bahamas, he had them go over the area again and then proceeded to clean out his own cabin of residue and paraphernalia. It was extremely unlikely that Bermuda customs would give them anything more than a cursory inspection, but if they found anything to arouse their suspicions, they'd tear the whole boat apart and he didn't know if they could withstand that type of search. By the time they were done the boat was clean except for one-half kilo Edward secreted in the walk-in freezer in an ice cream container for his own personal use.

"Bermuda Harbor Radio this is M/V White Lady, do you read me over?"

"White Lady, this is Bermuda Harbor Radio, please switch and answer channel 68 over?"

"Switching 68." Edward sat in the wheelhouse listening as his captain conversed and obtained permission to enter St. Georges Harbor.

"White Lady, Bermuda Harbor Radio, what is the size of your vessel, last port of call and number of passengers aboard, over?"

"Bermuda Harbor Radio, White Lady, we are 120 feet and our last port of call was Nassau, Bahamas. We have eight passengers including owner, captain and crew, over."

"Roger that. Please proceed directly to Customs and tie up on their outer dock, over."

Despite the cool 65-degree temperature on the bridge, Edward found himself sweating and poured himself a large vodka to help steady his nerves as they entered Town Cut. He desperately wanted the confidence that a few lines of coke would bring him but feared that a sharp customs agent might detect its increasingly obvious effects on his personality and opted for just the alcohol. If by some fluke of luck they were busted here in Bermuda that would be it, end of story, sayonara Eduardo. The Bermudans were nothing like the Bahamians or the Americans. Here, if they busted you, it was goodbye. No possibility of payoffs, no parole, just the rest of your natural life in a strict British prison surrounded by boring Brits.

"God, what a nightmare!" he thought to himself and emptied his glass as the captain brought them to a stop just off the edge of the dock. Hank exited the wheelhouse to the exterior controls on the wings of the bridge and slowly brought the White Lady alongside using a combination of main engines and bow thruster. Edward remained in the wheelhouse hidden for the time being behind the smoked glass of the bridge and nervously guzzled another drink and watched the activity on the pier.

Tory was scheduled to return that evening and Ryan was planning a special dinner for them all. Ryan, Jan and Willy were tying off their Zodiak on the opposite side of the quay as the White Lady docked at customs. Ryan recognized the boat immediately, recalling with distaste his last meeting with the owner. "I wonder what that asshole is doing here?" he thought uneasily. "You two go over and play on the cannons across from the White Horse Tavern for a while, I want to talk with someone," Ryan told the kids and walked over to one of the Customs agents standing near the front door of the building.

"Good morning Sergeant Sutton. How're you today?" Ryan asked.

"Same back to you Mr. Cunningham, I'm doing just fine." the agent replied.

Ryan gestured to the White Lady as he spoke. "I last saw that boat in Massachusetts and I'm curious, do you know where they're heading?"

"Haven't a clue. They indicated over the radio that they were in transit from Nassau, but I haven't been aboard yet to find out more. Why, are they friends of yours?"

Ryan snorted. "No. As a matter of fact the last time I saw them I nearly got into a fight with the owner. He almost ran me and my dog over in his tender and caused some problems in a friend's restaurant when he was there."

"Know anything about him or what his business is?" the agent asked.

"Not really, he's Latin and travels with a couple of bodyguard types. You know the kind; rich, cocky, a legend in his own mind. Seemed like a well-dressed scum bag to me," Ryan replied.

George chuckled. "I know the type. Thanks, we'll have a close look at him."

"Think nothing of it. No love lost between us and I know how much you folks like your peace and quiet."

"Quite so," the agent replied and shook Ryan's hand. Turning, Ryan walked off the pier to pick up Jan and Willy and then bring their groceries out to Parthenia.

Edward, still invisible to those on the pier behind the smoked glass of the White Lady's bridge, looked down in disbelief as Ryan conversed with the customs agent and pointed to White Lady. "What the fuck?" he muttered, immediately recognizing Ryan. He'd been high the night he and Ryan had confronted one another in Laura's restaurant, but he seldom forgot a face, especially one attached to someone who had challenged him. Edward's inflated ego did not allow anyone to get the better of him and Ryan had embarrassed him in front of Mr. Slade that evening. The captain re-entered the wheelhouse.

"We may have a problem Hank," Edward pointed to Ryan as he walked off the dock.

"How so?" the captain replied immediately. He was nervous enough as it was and Edward's words got his complete attention.

"Recognize him?" Edward motioned again to Ryan's retreating form. "No, never mind. You weren't there that evening," he said remembering that the captain had not been at dinner that night. For a moment he considered ordering their lines slipped and trying to depart the dock before the agents boarded, but quickly put it aside. They might get off the dock (as the agents weren't armed), but they'd never make it out of Bermuda waters before one of their coastal patrol boats chased them down. Besides, Ryan didn't know their business. Maybe he was just getting overly paranoid.

"It's just that I know that guy from our last stop in New England. Forget I said anything. He doesn't know anything about our real business. Just act natural and bring the inspectors to the main salon where we'll go over the paperwork with them." Edward turned and descended the short staircase down to the main salon.

The captain paused briefly and looked out the window as the crew swung their gangway into place. "Too late anyway," he thought to himself and gathered the file containing the White Lady's documentation and the passports of the crew and headed down the side stairway to the main deck where he cordially greeted the customs inspectors and invited them into the main salon. The interior of the White Lady was spectacular and the main salon where the customs inspectors entered was particularly so. Six master ship's carpenters had labored for almost nine months in this one 20-by-32-foot room at a cost of almost $1.5 million. Every cabinet, table, counter and bookcase was hand built of rosewood and Hawaiian koa, some of the pieces with brass inlays, others with olive burl veneer accents. All the upholstery was soft white leather and everything in the main salon was polished to a brilliant luster that was highlighted by dozens of recessed, low amperage mini lights. In the short interval before the customs inspectors were shown into the salon, Edward put on soft classical music, poured himself another drink and feigned the close of an important business conversation on the phone as they entered.

Edward got up off the couch and gestured to the three seats surrounding the couch. "Good morning gentlemen. Won't you please have a seat? I will have some coffee brought in." Although it was Edward's intent to intimidate the three black inspectors in the opulent salon and control the entire interview from the beginning, all three of the agents were well trained and quite used to boarding the many wealthy yachts that passed through Bermuda.

"Thank you, sir, but perhaps we could all have a seat at the table over there. The paperwork will go much faster."

George had taken an immediate dislike to Edward from his obvious attempt to flatter and control them and didn't even respond to the offer of coffee, although he was civil in his tone. This was as calculated as Edward's opening move.

"As you wish," Edward replied, annoyed that his initial advantage had been so quickly taken from him by the short, black inspector.

George settled into a chair at the head of the table and motioned his two men to seats on his left. Normally only one customs inspector would board a private yacht like White Lady unless they'd received a tip and planned on thoroughly searching it. Ryan's comments to him on the pier had piqued his interest in the vessel and if they were up to no good the psychological pressure of three inspectors might cause them to slip up.

"Henry, why don't you and Jules start the paperwork with the captain here. I will speak with the owner in the meantime," George turned to Edward. "I assume you are the owner sir?"

"Yes, and no," Edward replied.

"An interesting answer Mr. ....?"

"Rodriguez."

"Rodriguez, yes quite. Please explain yes and no," George replied.

"Certainly, perhaps you could tell me who I have the privilege of addressing?" Edward had to make a conscious effort to keep the sarcasm out of his voice. The jungle bunny in front of him was not at all deferential and he found his perfect English and steady stare discomforting.

"Sergeant George Sutton."

Edward made one last attempt to take control of the meeting. "Yes, as I was saying George..."

"Mr. Rodriguez, I would prefer it if you would address me as Sergeant Sutton. I'm a little old fashioned and the missus and a few close friends are the only ones on this island who address me as George.

"Sergeant Sutton, of course, my apologies. As I started to say initially, yes and no. What I meant by 'no' was, I am not *the* owner. However, 'yes,' I am *an* owner. You see, the White Lady is owned by a corporation of which I am a substantial shareholder. That is why the answer is not a simple one," Edward wanted to finish his statement with the addendum, "You stupid, fucking, banana eating ape," but restrained himself.

George knew he'd annoyed Edward but that was his intention. "And where is this Corporation based and what is their business?" he replied.

"We are a Grand Cayman corporation as I'm sure you'll note on the paperwork and have varied interests worldwide. We buy things like shopping malls, other corporations and on occasion small countries when the opportunity arises."

Edward smiled at his little joke. George did not. Already his guard was up with the two additional inspectors and what seemed like an inordinate amount of interest on the part of the jig in front of him. He briefly let his mind wander to the fantasy of what it would be like to have a 'wet' workout with the impertinent little prick down in the engine room.

"I'm sure that must be very nice for you Mr. Rodriguez. What may I ask is the purpose of your visit to Bermuda?" George asked.

"Pleasure, we have no business planned here in Bermuda and are just passing through."

Sergeant Sutton's interest was heightened by the Cayman Corp. ownership of White Lady. In his experience there were few legitimate Cayman Island corporations. At best, the man in front of him was a tax cheat who laundered money outside the auspices of his government. At worst, he was a drug smuggler or an arms dealer. George thought all three types very low in the food chain and at that moment decided to make things difficult for the cocky gentleman in front of him.

"Jules, please pass me Mr. Rodriguez's passport." Jules did as ordered and passed him Edward's passport. George began to methodically leaf through it, page by page, taking his time and making mental notes of all the entries. The room was silent as he flipped through it except for Jules's pen on the custom's form and the occasional cycling of the air conditioning.

"Mr. Rodriguez, when exactly do you find time to work? It appears from your passport that you do nothing but travel between the U.S., Europe, Colombia and let's see, oh yes, the Bahamas."

Edward shrugged his shoulders. "What can I say? I have business interests in all those countries. Most of my travel is business related."

"Let's see. The most recent entry is from Nassau six days ago; pardon me for asking but I've always been intrigued by the world of high finance. What exactly were you buying on this trip?" George smiled and wondered if Mr. Rodriguez would squirm a little at his direct question.

Edward paused before answering quickly trying to think of a plausible answer and then caught himself. "Sergeant Sutton, I'm not applying for citizenship. I merely stopped to refuel my ship and enjoy your lovely island for a few days. Do you really care about the details of my business?"

George kept his expression neutral and held Edwards stare until Edward finally turned away. He was annoyed with the man's arrogance and decided at that moment that they'd played enough cat and mouse.

"You're absolutely right Mr. Rodriguez. I guess I really don't have any interest in your business," He paused. "Unless of course it may perchance be in contravention of the laws of Bermuda. Do you have anything you wish to declare? This would include fruits and vegetables, animals, cash in excess of $10,000, guns of any kind, and of course drugs, both prescription or illegal?"

Edward stared hard again at Sergeant Sutton, barely concealing his contempt. "Yes, I'm sure we have a number of items we'd like to declare. We have several weapons aboard which I'll have the captain show you, and various prescription drugs. I'm sure you're aware of the dangers a wealthy man such as myself faces in this violent world. The Captain holds an Interpol permit to be in possession of the guns. I'm sure you will find all the paperwork in order."

"We'll see. Captain would you please call your crew back in here one by one. Jules, you and Elliot interview them and take a complete inventory of prescription drugs." George turned back to Edward.

"Are you in possession of any illegal drugs Mr. Rodriguez?" He was gratified to see Edward blink, just once, at his direct question.

"No, of course not Sergeant."

"Jules, on second thought, cancel the crew interviews. I'd like to conduct a thorough search of Mr. Rodriguez's vessel first."

Edward's heart rate jumped 50 points. "Sergeant Sutton, do you really think that's necessary. Have I done something to annoy you?"

"Annoy me? No, I think not. Just call it a feeling. You know how we custom's types are. Occasionally on a vessel with an international crew like yours, the captain and owner are unaware of everything that goes on. I wouldn't think to impeach your honesty, but I do find that by doing occasional random searches word passes quickly among the crews of other yachts. It has a strong deterrent effect on them. You know how strongly we feel about illegal drugs here in Bermuda. Now, please call the rest of your crew back into the salon here and hold them until we've finished."

White Lady's crew reassembled in the main salon and George gathered his own men on the afterdeck to plan the search and assign areas of responsibility. He also called over to the local search and rescue station to request a diver, as Customs did not keep one at the ready. He wanted to have a good look below the waterline of the White Lady. Just two years before. he'd discovered several hundred pounds of heroin in the lead keel of a sailboat. Granted; he'd reason to strongly suspect them from their appearance on an Interpol flyer, but if he hadn't been thorough, it would have escaped him. As he'd looked through the bilge of that particular vessel, he'd noticed a slight discoloration of the lead on the top of the keel. Acting on intuition he'd ordered a large power drill and drill bit and augured into the suspicious area. He recalled with satisfaction the long curly-cues of lead as they spiraled up the bit and then the sudden lack of resistance as the bit plunged through into the soft white center of the illegal cargo; the lead-gray, curly-cues were suddenly replaced by white powder as the bit continued to spin. Those men would never know freedom again. He certainly wouldn't lose any sleep if the same thing were to happen to this pompous ass, he thought to himself.

George had his men start their search in the forepeak, methodically working their way aft. As was his custom, instead of joining them in their detailed search peering into cabinets and looking beneath floorboards, he moved around the ship trying to get a more general feel, looking at things like design, function and proportion. Obviously, they weren't going to find 100 neatly stacked bales of marijuana in one of the closets or storerooms, so he went through the ship with the eye of a marine architect, looking for any trees out of place in the forest. His men were quite competent and motivated, and he knew they'd find the simple and obvious. He searched for the complex and devious. One of George's favorite tools was a simple tape measure and he looked for violations of the primary rule of yacht design, that space, is never wasted. Vessels of White Lady's size frequently cost in excess of $100,000 a foot to build, and designers had a purpose for every dimension. Find a few extra inches in a bulkhead, an empty or unnecessary tank, or any item that does not serve a very specific purpose and you have as likely as not found a hiding place. One of the main reasons that he'd requested a diver was that over the years several of the wealthier more sophisticated smugglers he'd busted had tried welding underwater containers of various dimensions to the undersides of their vessels. This necessitated hauling the ship at both ends of the trip to load and extract their cargoes, but money was not an issue to these types and they were mistaken in their belief that nothing was ever looked at below the waterline.

Edward paced the main salon swilling vodka and cursing the stranger from Massachusetts who he was convinced had put Customs onto them. As fate had it, Ryan and the children chose that time to motor past White Lady in the Zodiac on their way out to Parthenia. Edward looked down on them as they passed and turned to Paulo.

"I don't care what it takes, but if we get out of this thing, I want his ass. Do you hear me? Find out where he lives and everything there is to know about him. That is going to be one sorry cocksucker who will wish he had never, ever, fucked with me!"

Manuel listened to Edward rant on about the gringo as Paulo climbed the short staircase to the bridge and followed Ryan's progress across the harbor with a pair of binoculars, paying particular attention to Jan. "So young and tender," Paulo thought to himself. Eventually they pulled alongside Parthenia and started to unload their groceries. Edward would be pleased that he'd discovered so quickly where they lived. He rubbed himself through his greasy, soiled shorts fantasizing about the things he might do to Jan's young body before going below to report to Edward.

***

Ryan worried about Tory during her trip to the mainland and was grateful for the responsibility and distraction that the children provided. Her absence also enabled him to get closer to both of them and understand Jan's serious and often withdrawn moods. At the age of seven she'd assumed responsibility for both her brother's and her mother's welfare, a heavy burden for one with such small shoulders and it was all he could do sometimes to restrain himself from gathering her up in his arms and pledging his devotion and lifelong protection. He wished he could exorcise all her demons and felt a powerful loyalty to the strong little girl who had kept his new family together during Tory's addiction. Three nights earlier he'd awakened to the sound of her softly crying in the bunk across the cabin and had gotten up and gone over and sat down on the edge of her bunk.

"What's wrong Jan?" he'd asked.

She turned away at first. Old habits were hard to break and she was not accustomed to sharing or letting anyone see her pain. She'd known intuitively that if other adults found out about Tory's addictions and their home life, that she and Willy might be separated from her. As a result, it was only in the isolation and black of night when no one else could see her that she allowed herself to feel, and breathe, and cry. She'd always been hesitant about making real friends (for fear of them finding out about her home life) and as a result had developed a rich fantasy life. In these early morning hours, she'd frequently read to herself at the kitchen table and have conversations with imaginary friends between trips to check on Tory and Willy. Some nights, however, the cold blackness that pressed in against the windows was so total that it would overwhelm her with its oppressive emptiness, and she'd shiver alone in a blanket on the couch, her heart fluttering like a small scared bird.

She'd been sleeping better since Tory had gotten sober and they'd all been reunited, but this was the first time that she'd been separated from Tory since her discharge from the halfway house and some of the old demons had come back to haunt her on this night. Ryan was different than all the other adults she'd ever known and she sensed that he cared for Tory very much. She also knew that he cared for her and Willy and that he could be trusted. His care and concern had taken some of the pressure off her in recent weeks and their time in Bermuda had been as carefree a time as any she could recall. It felt wonderful to have someone share the responsibility that she'd heretofore borne alone (even if they were silent partners). She decided to take a chance and let him in some more.

She turned towards him and wiped the tears from her face with the back of her hand. "I was just thinking about Mom. She's not used to being alone and I worry about her."

"She's not alone Jan, she's with your grandmother."

"I know, but I mean she's not with us. You, me and Willy."

Ryan knew exactly what she meant and was flattered that she'd included him in the short, exclusive list. Jan had always partially blamed her grandmother for their separation and considered her an outsider. Ryan leaned back against the bulkhead at the head of the bunk and put his arm around her.

"Yea, I know what you mean. I miss her too. I think she's doing OK. I know you've had a tough time of it over the last few years and your Mom knows it too. I also know that she loves you very much and is working as hard as she can to heal herself. For what it's worth, I think she's going to make it."

"I hope so Ryan. I don't know what I'd do without her." Jan pulled the covers tight around her and turned so her head was resting against the side of Ryan's chest and fell back asleep within minutes.

Ryan lay there for several more minutes with one arm around her, gently stroking her forehead until he was sure she was soundly asleep and then eased off the bunk and returned to his own. As he lay there in the dark he mulled over the interdependence of the three. He hoped his relationship with Tory would leave Jan feeling less responsible and that she might be able to recover and enjoy a few years of her stolen childhood before entering the maze of teenage adolescence. Tory's nightly phone calls had helped quell her fears, but he knew that there were a lot of unresolved issues between Tory and her grandmother. She'd indicated over the phone that she'd made amends to her Grandmother, but he also knew Tory was feeling isolated and alone and he was glad she was going to return later that day.

***

George's men methodically worked their way aft over the next hour, and except for the rather extensive collection of arms that were inventoried aboard the ship, they found nothing else contravening Bermuda law. The captain did in fact possess a valid Interpol license for the weapons, but their presence and number only served to heighten George's suspicions about the White Lady and her crew. They'd finished up the forward two-thirds of their search missing the cocaine that Edward had carefully packed in the ice cream container and were about to start in the engine room and machinery spaces below.

"Jules, I want you and Henry to pull up every deck plate in this whole area and examine every square inch of bilge. Don't overlook anything. Remember, if there's something here, it will probably be in the most difficult place of all to get to. I also want every tank, line, and piece of machinery down here checked for function. Start by bringing the engineer down from the bridge and have him fire up everything down here; the engines; mains, generators, compressor, desalinator, all of them. If it's mechanical I want you to establish that it functions. Understand?"

"Yes, Sergeant Sutton," Jules replied and set off to the bridge to fetch the engineer after ordering Henry to start taking up deck plates.

Several years before, George had read about an offshore tug that had been boarded and searched by the U.S. Coast Guard off the coast of New Jersey. While searching that vessel, a sharp officer off the cutter had noted that one of the main engines in the engine room was cold. When he questioned the Lebanese captain about it the captain had become agitated. Acting on impulse the officer had directed his men to remove one of the valve covers. Inside the engine they found over two hundred pounds of heroin. In that case every internal part had been removed and replaced with neatly packed bricks of the drug. While George waited for Jules to return with the engineer, he continued to walk the machine space, looking, measuring with his eyes, and following the miles of pipes and wires that crisscrossed the space between the various engines, tanks, and compartments looking for anything that appeared superfluous, out of place, or non-functioning. He paused at the port side wing tank that had had the fuel blockage in it several days earlier.

"Henry, bring your light over here. There's something I want to look at." George directed.

He climbed down into the bilge and shined the beam around the area of the main primary filters where several nights earlier the engineer and Manuel had labored for so long to restore the flow of fuel to the ship's engines. "See how clean it is in this area," and pointed to the area of bilge immediately below the filters. George reached out with his hand and tapped the tank tentatively in several places and then directed the flashlight beam up underneath the cramped bulkhead where he could see that the dust and grime normally found on engine room surfaces had been disturbed on top of the tank, as if someone had recently crawled back into that confined space on top of the tank. A smile came to George's normally impassive face.

"Come on down here Henry, I want you to have a look at something."

Henry did as requested and looked where George was pointing. "Could be something Sergeant Sutton, would you like me to have a look back there?"

"Indeed, I would. See if there is an access plate into that tank."

Henry took the light from his superior and wedged himself up into the tight space and crawled forward to the access port. "You're right Sergeant Sutton. There is an access port back here and the nuts securing it have been turned recently."

"Right," George thought for a moment. "OK, come on out. I want to bring Mr. Rodriguez below for this. I would like to see his reaction when I tell him that we're going to have a look inside."

As George and Henry climbed up out of the bilge, Jules returned with the engineer.

"Hold him here for a moment Jules while I fetch Mr. Rodriguez. I have some questions I would like to ask them both together. Then we can run the engines." George climbed back on deck and then entered the main salon. The talk immediately stopped as he entered.

"Mr. Rodriguez, would you come below with me please. There are some questions I'd like to ask you concerning one of your storage tanks."

At George's words, Edward paled noticeably and took several moments to collect his thoughts. George stood in front of him, smiling at his discomfort, relishing the moment. Edward's mind raced in those few uncomfortable seconds and he wondered how on earth the smug customs inspector could have possibly discovered their hiding place unless one of the crew had talked. He'd have to bluff it out though.

"Sergeant, I can't imagine what help I could be in the engine room. My world is one of paperwork and telephone conversations and I doubt I've been in the engine room twice in the entire time that I've owned this ship. Surely the engineer is much better qualified to answer your questions than I."

"That's probably true sir, but please indulge me anyway," George replied. He had no intention of exposing a possibly illegal cache without being able to see the look on the arrogant Colombian's face. The two of them exited the salon. Manuel, Paulo, Hank and the other two crew exchanged anxious glances.

"Sergeant, I don't understand your fixation with me and my ship. What have we done to arouse your suspicions so?"

"Mr. Rodriguez, man to man?"

"Yes, certainly."

"I don't like you. I don't like rich arrogant foreigners with multimillion-dollar yachts and vague answers concerning their business. I especially don't like people who lead a lifestyle that requires that they travel around with bodyguards and an arsenal of automatic weapons. I can only assume that you must piss off a lot of people to fear so for your life. I don't really know what your business is. You may smuggle drugs. You may be an illegal arms dealer. For all I know you may work for your government. But all that said, I think it's a safe bet that in some way, you make other people's lives miserable. I don't know how, *yet*. But I suspect that we shall find out in the next few minutes."

Edward didn't have an immediate reply and followed George down the stairs into the engine room fearing the worst. As they walked through the bulkhead into the engine room he was surprised and relieved to see that the deck plates over the water tanks remained in place and that the Engineer and the other customs agents were all standing around the forward end of the engine room near the main fuel tank. He risked a quick look into the engineer's eyes hoping for some sign that everything was in fact OK. Although brief, he got it. When Sergeant Sutton had come to the salon for him and indicated he, "had some questions concerning storage tanks," he hadn't said which ones. He'd just assumed that the customs agent was talking about the false water tank. Some of his earlier confidence returned.

"Sergeant Sutton, now that you have me down here, please explain how you expect me to be of any help in this wild goose chase?"

This was not the reaction that George had hoped for. "We noticed during the course of our inspection that this tank was recently accessed through the inspection port and we thought you might be able to shed some light on it."

"I keep telling you, I know nothing about this engine room. Ask the engineer. I'm sure he has an explanation."

Edward turned to his man. "Roberto, have you recently had occasion to enter or tamper with this tank?"

"Si, Senor Edward. Don't you remember the engine trouble we had last week in the Bahamas?"

"Yes, I remember some inconvenience." Of course, Edward remembered perfectly but continued to play the role of naive owner.

"Well, it was in this tank that I believed we had a block of some kind. I had the inspection cover off when I was trying to figure out why we weren't getting any fuel to the main filters," Roberto replied.

"See Sergeant, there you have it, a simple answer to a simple problem. Some sort of blockage was in this tank and he gained entrance to free it. Does that answer your question?"

"That could be Senor Rodriguez, but I don't believe I will ever have another night's sleep unless I ascertain that this tank is being used for the contents it was designed for."

George turned to Jules. "Let's look inside, shall we?" He turned to the Engineer. "While my man is removing the cover to that tank would you please be so kind as to fire up every engine in this space. I would like to ascertain that they are all functioning properly."

Edward made an exasperated sound. "Sergeant, is it really necessary that I stay below for all of this? I have other things I would like to attend to."

"Sit, Senor Rodriguez. We won't be that much longer."

Edward gestured with his hand for the engineer to go ahead and do as Sergeant Sutton had ordered. "Do as he asks Roberto. Obviously the Sergeant will not leave us until he is satisfied."

George followed Roberto around the engine room, watching closely as he started every engine on the ship until everything below was running as Jules removed the nuts on the fuel tank access plate. Despite this, he still had the feeling that he was overlooking something. Ship, Cayman registry, Colombian citizen, firearms on board; all the signs were there that there was something to find. But where, and what?

Jules crawled out of the cramped space above the fuel tank and motioned to George across the room indicating that he'd taken the lid off.

"OK Roberto, you may shut down the engines. I can't hear myself think in here!" George yelled.

As the engines whined down George walked the short distance over to Jules. "Anything?"

"Hard to tell. I can only see several inches into the tank due to the cloudiness of the fuel." He replied.

"All right, look around and see if there isn't something we can feel around in there with."

The engineer volunteered. "Sergeant, when we had the blockage before I used a plumbers snake. Would that help?"

"Yes, I suppose that would. Jules, take him up on is offer." George ordered.

Jules climbed back into the space above the tank and took the proffered snake from Roberto, inserted it into the tank and started fishing around in a random manner. George placed his ear up to the tank and could hear the snake as it made contact with the walls. "Damn, what am I missing?" He wondered.

"Sergeant, are you satisfied yet?" Edward asked in a bored patronizing tone.

George got to his feet and looked him in the eye. "It doesn't appear as though there's anything in this tank other than fuel. We do, however, still have several areas I want to look over."

Edward held his stare for several moments betraying nothing. "Very well Sergeant, have it your way. May I please return to the salon? Surely you don't require my presence any longer?"

"Yes Mr. Rodriguez, you may return to the salon. Please instruct your crew to remain aboard until I've completed my inspection and we release you all."

"Very well," Edward replied and walked briskly through the bulkhead and up onto the deck.

George ordered his men to put the deck plates back down in the forward part of the engine room and pull up the ones in the aft section. He was disappointed but had not yet given up and jumped down into the bilge as soon as the plates were removed. He stood looking at the three water tanks.

"Roberto, how many gallons of fresh water per day does your desalinization plant manufacture?"

"Eight hundred, mas o menos." Roberto replied.

"How many gallons in each of these tanks?"

"I believe they're five hundred each"

"You must use a great deal of freshwater aboard this vessel." He thought for a moment more. "I assume they are all functioning?"

Roberto's heart rate rose several points. "Si, Senor Sergeant."

"They all contain water and are attached to the system?"

A few new beads off sweat appeared on Roberto's brow. "Why yes, to the best of my knowledge."

"Are you not the engineer and responsible for everything in this room?"

"Si."

"So why are you unsure?" George pushed the engineer hard, trying to fluster him.

"Well, I'm not. I meant to say that yes, everything works."

George shone his light over the top of all three tanks and then came back to the center one where the cocaine was stored. He'd noticed that of the three, only this one seemed to have any kind of access other than the feeder pipes, crossover hoses, and outlet spigots on each. He bent over the top of the tank and looked back towards the welded plate. Although the dirt and grime did not appear to have been disturbed in the recent past he backed out of the tight space and looked at Roberto again.

"Why does this tank have a welded access plate whereas the others are bolted?"

"I don't know Sergeant. These tanks were all installed prior to my hiring on. I did not know that they differed."

"Jules, pass me a screwdriver please."

Jules did as he was told and George undid the hose clamps that secured the outflow hoses at the base of each tank. Then he pulled each hose off, starting with the port, then center, then starboard tank. Water gushed from each of the spigots as it was opened. Roberto was almost beside himself trying to control his panic. All three tanks were equipped with crossover hoses that theoretically kept them at equal levels. If the water stopped gushing from the center tank before the other two tanks, he knew the Sergeant would figure out their hiding place.

He couldn't contain himself. "Sergeant, you're going to waste all our fresh water. Can't you see that all three tanks are exactly what they look like?"

George was torn. It appeared that all three were working tanks. What had he missed?

"Yes, it would appear so Roberto," George reached down and turned off first the starboard, then the port, and finally the center tank spigots then climbed up out of the bilge. Roberto almost passed out with relief as the last one was turned off.

George climbed up out of the bilge scratching his head. "Jules, put those hoses back on and finish up in here, then put a wire and seal on their arms locker. I'll be back in the office finishing the paperwork. When you're done, you can pick up the paperwork and release the ship." Depressed that he hadn't caught them in an illegal act he walked back to the office making a silent vow to keep an eye on the ship during their stay.

Ten minutes later George released White Lady and they pulled away from the dock. Edward was on bridge with the captain, Paulo, and Manuel. "That was too close, too fucking close!" he yelled. "I don't know what that meddling prick said to that black bastard, but I was serious, I want you to find out everything you can about him. Nobody fucks with me, especially a little cocksucker like him!"

"Like I told you before Senor Edward, it appears that he is staying aboard a boat just over there on the other side of the harbor," Paulo replied.

Edward turned to where he was pointing. "OK Hank, I want you to anchor close enough so that we can keep an eye on him, but not so close that we're in his face. I want to know who is with him, where he goes, everything about him. Is that understood?"

All three nodded and Edward went below to fish his cocaine out of the freezer. Manuel and Paulo talked between themselves and set up a schedule so that one of them would always be on the bridge to watch the Parthenia. They also ordered the smaller Zodiac tender launched so that they could follow him unobtrusively if he crossed the harbor again.

Ryan spent the afternoon with Jan and Willy in Mike and Jill's kitchen taking advantage of the counter space and electric conveniences that had no place in Parthenia's small galley. He was as excited about Tory's return as both children and the three of them made fresh sourdough bread and a flourless chocolate cappuccino torte in advance of the meal. They also peeled and deveined several pounds of shrimp and set that to marinate in a mixture of Caribbean spices. They'd grill the shrimp over charcoal on the stern hibachi on Parthenia. Ryan felt like a teenager as the afternoon progressed and wondered if things would be the same between Tory and him after their 11-day separation. In his excitement and anticipation, they left for the airport an hour earlier than necessary.

Paulo noted their movement off Parthenia ashore early in the afternoon. It had not occurred to him that they might also have a shore base. Edward ordered Manuel to rush into St. George's and rent a scooter. When Ryan and the children departed for the airport, Manuel followed at a distance after being alerted on his hand-held radio that they were on the move.

Tory was introspective for most of the flight, lost in her memories of Pops and her past life. It wasn't until final approach that her thoughts turned to Ryan and the children and what lay ahead for all of them. When she emerged from customs she was fairly exploding with anticipation. Jan spotted her first.

"There she is!" Jan shouted.

Tory spotted them right away and rushed forward not knowing whom to hug first. She needn't have worried as all three of them simultaneously found a body part to hang onto and she was fairly smothered with affection.

"God it's good to see you guys. Did you miss me?" Tory stepped back to look at the three of them, sun tanned and smiling in front of her.

"Not really, but anything would be better than Ryan," Jan offered.

"Why you little shit!" Ryan sputtered back.

"Shit! That's worth 50 cents," Willy gleefully noted.

"Damn. I forgot!" Ryan said, again without thinking. "I decided to clean up my language and I told Willy that I'd start paying him again for cuss words."

"Damn. That's worth a quarter," Willy ticked off.

"I'll bet he's making a fortune!" Tory said fairly beaming with joy.

"Yeah mom, and I get a buck for a fuck!" Willy added with a serious expression.

Tory burst out laughing and reached out and ruffled his hair. "A buck for a fuck? That's great sweetheart. I guess I'll really have to watch myself with all this incentive floating around." Tory took a step back and looked admiringly at both children. "You two look great. But I can see I have some catching up to do in the tanning department."

"Yeah, the weather's been great for the last five days and we got quite a bit done on the boat. These two helped me varnish the cockpit combings and we scrubbed the bottom." Ryan replied.

"Did Willy really help?" Tory asked.

"Yup. He did a lot of the water line."

"And I did it without a life jacket mom."

"What? Really?" Tory looked up at Ryan for confirmation.

"He speaks the truth. Willy can now swim without a life jacket. He held onto the dinghy some while he worked but it's true, he's now a swimmer."

Tory knelt next to him. "I am so proud of you. That's great."

"And I'm going to learn how to jump off the side like Jan!"

"I'm sure you are. Jeez, I go away for 11 days and you guys are all grown up. I don't know what you need me for."

"You can still cook and clean up after us mom," Jan suggested.

"Yeah right. Well, what do you say we get outta here so I can get out of my arctic outfit and into a bathing suit? And you, young man, can show me what a Tarzan you are."

Willy looked up. "What's a Tarzan?"

"Oh, he was a guy who lived over in Africa who swam a lot and liked to wrestle alligators and stuff," Tory replied.

Willy puffed up his little chest. "Yeah, I could do that."

Manuel followed them from a distance as they left the terminal building. When they turned into Mike and Jill's driveway, he continued past and pulled into the woods nearby and reported back to Paulo.

Tory stopped at the house just long enough to say hello to Mike and Jill then they all rowed out to the boat for a swim.

Paulo closely watched them all closely through the binoculars, particularly Jan.

Edward came onto the bridge several minutes later and grabbed the glasses out of Paulo's hands.

"I see my friend is back. How touching, a little afternoon swim with the family." An idea began to form in Edward's head as he watched Tory and Ryan swimming side by side and playing with one another.

"Perhaps the best way to send a message to our friend would be through his family. What do you think Paulo?"

Paulo was quick to reply. "Yes, an excellent idea Senor Edward. Perhaps something with the little girl?" Paulo's lust was thick in the air as he asked the question.

"Yes, I suppose that's a possibility. Let's learn a little more about them first. Are you in contact with Manuel?"

"Si, senor. We're using the scrambled VHF. Would you like to talk with him?"

"Yeah, get him."

Paulo picked up the hand-held. "You there Manuel?"

"Yes, I'm here. What is it?" Manuel immediately replied.

Edward grabbed the radio out of his hand. "Manuel, do you have good cover there?"

"Yes, there is a small hill on the opposite side of the road from their driveway entrance and no one to notice me. Why?"

"I just want to keep an eye on them till they go to sleep. If they leave the boat again I'll have Paulo give you a call."

"No problem as long as Paulo watches. There's a small cafe down the road I can grab a bite at later if they are up long."

Edward handed the radio back to Paulo. "Remember, I don't want anything to happen to them yet. Just watch."

Paulo nodded and returned to leering at Jan's young body in the fading light.

Chapter 10

Ryan, Tory, Jan and Willy swam until the clouds turned pastel and gradually intensified to a vivid crimson color. The air cooled several degrees and the four of them headed below to put on dry clothes and prepare dinner. Ryan was the last to go below and looked back across the harbor in the fading light to where the White Lady swung gently at her anchor. Her decks were softly lit with courtesy lights around the deck perimeter, but her smoked windows were dark and betrayed no sign of life aboard the huge yacht. A shiver washed over him at the sight of the boat and he headed down the companionway ladder to his own warmly lit cabin.

Tory and Ryan quickly eased back into a warm, relaxed, familiarity and lay on deck with Clifton talking for several hours after the children had gone to sleep. Clifton didn't seem to want to let Tory out of his sight and would alternatively lay his saliva thick jaw in her lap and roll on his back all the while rubbing against her until Ryan finally sent him back to the cockpit so that the two of them could be alone.

"I missed you, a lot," Ryan offered.

"I know. Me too." Tory paused and thought for a while. "You know, it's strange. The whole time I was back there I had this horrible feeling in my gut, and it wasn't just because Pops was dying. It was more like that whole geographic area and all the people I saw were somehow a part of everything negative that had made me. All those things and people are still there, and it was very uncomfortable at times. Everyone stuffs everything there. I mean sure, people came by to express their "grief" and say how sorry they were, but it was if everyone was following some script and I felt like shaking them and saying, *"What, do, you, really, mean?* What's going on in your head?"

"And then of course there were the ones who hid behind their coffee cups after the service, smiling at me across the room but whispering among each other about my sad situation. You know the talk, what a disappointment I must be, and don't forget 'the poor children'! I mean who the hell made them the Andy's and Aunt damn Bea's of Mayberry?"

"Don't sugar coat your feelings." Ryan said with a straight face.

"Shit! I'm glad Willy's not still awake; I'd owe him a fortune. I'm sorry, I didn't mean to go off on you, but it was difficult, and every negative feeling I've ever had about myself flooded right back when I was there. No wonder I turned into a damn drug addict."

Ryan listened patiently until she finished. "Well, you made it back safe and sound and you know something?"

"What?"

"You were there for your grandmother and you kept your sobriety. That's the only thing that matters. I'm sure your Grandfather was looking down and proud of you."

"Thanks, that helps. Tory's intense expression softened, she smiled and she reached for one of his hands. "You're pretty special."

"You are too."

They embraced and quietly made love on deck several minutes later.

Paulo continued to watch the two of them through the binoculars after darkness fell. Although details were difficult to make out with only a quarter moon up there was still enough ambient light that he could tell by the rhythmic nature of their movements, what the two of them were doing. He continued to watch them as they made love and enjoyed the thought that the two enjoyed so much passion. Any plan to hurt the interfering gringo would definitely have to include the women.

Chapter 11

Tory woke early before the others the next morning and swam for almost 20 minutes before re-boarding Parthenia. The 11 days at her grandmother's had left her feeling sedentary and unfit and it felt good to stretch her muscles. After climbing back aboard she crossed into the cockpit and demurely slid out of her bathing suit with her back to the shore and began to rinse the salt off with the freshwater hose. At the sound of the freshwater pressure pump cycling, Ryan stirred and after several moments poked his head up through the cockpit hatch to see what was going on. The sun had yet to rise further than the barrier island that separated them from the sea, and the harbor was quiet and suffused with the still soft light of a sleepy sun. Tory's eyes were closed and her head was tilted back as she rinsed off and Ryan stood there halfway up the ladder, saying nothing, feeling like the luckiest man on earth and stared at her as the water washed off her head, over her pink nipples and finally down her flat stomach and short cropped pudendum. He wished he could stop time right there.

"Has anyone told you how beautiful you are yet this morning?" he asked quietly.

Tory smiled with her eyes still closed and wiped the water from them before turning off the hose. Then she turned slowly to him. "No, not that I can recall."

"Well, you are and I was just thinking how lucky I am."

Tory looked unashamedly down at her own body. "Thanks, I'd be lying if I said it wasn't important that you find me irresistible," then she added, almost absently, "Although I could use a shave." And moved her legs slightly apart and casually traced her fingers over her small mound and the downy hair that was starting to grow back. "It's starting to look more like a Georgia peach than a plum."

"Christ, I'm starting to sport wood here. How about a quickie before the kids get up?"

Tory sighed in an exaggerated fashion. "So like a man, no romance, no foreplay. A quickie indeed! Just think about baseball or the IRS and stuff that thing back in your shorts?"

Ryan sucked in a breath through clenched teeth and started to climb into the cockpit.

"I'm serious Ryan," Tory laughed and reached for the towel next to her, quickly wrapped it around her lower body and sat down to comb out her hair.

Ryan sat down next to her and put his arm around her.

Tory laughed at his expression. "Really Ryan, would you please show some restraint. You're like a dolphin or something!"

"A dolphin?"

"Yes, a dolphin. I read somewhere that dolphins are the horniest creatures on earth and that they mate eight to 10 times a day."

"Lucky them," Ryan replied.

"No really. Don't get yourself all worked up. We've got a lot to do today"

Ryan sighed. "OK, but promise me we can try all sorts of new and degrading acts later?"

"I certainly will not. Christ, what happened to groping around in the dark and a good straight missionary type screw anyway?" she replied.

"What are we doing today anyway, I forget?"

"I know, you poor baby. Your schedule is so hectic. Well, for one, you told Willy you would teach him how to dive this morning, and two, you promised Mike you would help him rig his sailing dinghy over at The Dinghy Club this afternoon. I plan on going to that noontime Narcotics Anonymous meeting in Hamilton. I haven't been to a meeting in two weeks and really feel like I could use one. Can you take the kids with you to Mike's for the afternoon?"

"Sure, no problem."

Paulo was immediately on the hand-held and alerted Manuel to Tory's movement when she left on her scooter for Hamilton later that morning. Manuel was still on the hillock across from Mike and Jill's driveway. When she emerged from the driveway a few minutes later Manuel was ready and followed her at a prudent distance on his own scooter for the entire 10-mile trip into Hamilton. After she parked Manuel continued to follow her on foot. She went into a church. Manuel followed and after waiting a minute peered cautiously into the chapel. No one was there. He went to the front of the chapel worried he'd lost her but heard voices coming up from the bottom of a stairwell and descended the stairs to some sort of meeting room.

Tory had taken a seat near the podium at the front of the room and Manuel (after figuring out that it was a public meeting of some kind) took a seat in the back. The person sitting next to him immediately sensed his discomfort and leaned over.

"Welcome friend. Are you new to the program."

Manuel had heard the opening invocation of, "Narcotics Anonymous is a fellowship of men and women who share their experience, strength, and hope with others..." and tried to think of what to say so as not to attract unwanted attention. Nothing came so he just grunted back an unintelligible reply and kept his eyes forward hoping that the individual would leave him alone. After the reading of the preamble, the 12-Steps and the promises of NA, the chairperson called the first of four speakers for the hour. Manuel listened to the stories as he furtively kept an eye on Tory and was mesmerized by the unfortunate things that had happened to the speakers during their days using drugs.

"I started drinking and doing drugs when I was 12 and never thought it was a problem," One speaker related. "All my friends were doing it, and even when I started using and drinking in the morning years later, I still didn't think I had a problem. I was just having a good time or steadying my nerves I told myself. Then one evening I was driving my wife and two children back from a company cookout and I missed a stop sign." He stopped for a moment to collect himself and then in a choking voice continued.

"I woke up in the hospital several days later; my wife and one of my children were killed in the crash," he sobbed quietly for a few moments in the quiet room and then continued, "My wife's parents got custody of my remaining child and I served four years in jail. Still, I didn't stop using and used both in prison and afterwards for an additional three years. There was just so much pain. I had lost everything humanly possible. I was powerless over drugs and alcohol. And rather than soothing my pain, they were the source of everything painful in my life, but I just couldn't make that connection."

He paused again then continued. "I've been sober now nine months and I know that I will never recover the people and things I've lost but through this program and the people in it I at least have hope that I'll have a future. Thanks."

Towards the end of the meeting the chairperson asked if anyone had a burning desire to share before she closed it. Tory put up her hand and was recognized by the chairperson.

"Hi, my name is Tory and I'm also a drug addict and an alcoholic. I've been sober now for about 14 months and I owe it all to this program. I'm grateful. I just went through a tough two weeks with the death of a relative who I was very close to and without the tools that this program gave me I don't think I could have made it. If it was the old days I would have used and stumbled through the days high as a kite and full of self-pity spending all my time trying to score more coke from my dealer and sneaking drinks all the while being nothing but a further source of worry for the ones that I was trying to support."

"I didn't have to do that this time. I also lost a great deal like the gentleman who spoke before me, but I've been lucky in that today I have my children back and I've fallen in love with another sober person. I'm no longer a slave to the crack pipe and the bottle and I have choices, wonderful choices and opportunities. God willing, I can stay sober and rebuild the trust of my children and have a healthy relationship with someone else. I would just say to the speaker before me, hang in there, it gets better. Thank you."

Not accustomed to hearing people speak honestly about themselves or their feelings Manuel was moved by Tory's story and all the others he heard. It did not escape him that as a drug smuggler he was directly responsible for the drugs that they addicted themselves to. He'd never really thought about it before and feelings of guilt washed over him. "Is this the person I was brought up to be?" he asked himself for the second time that month.

At the conclusion of the meeting he again followed Tory as she did some grocery shopping in Hamilton and later followed her back to Mike and Jill's. He regained his hiding place behind the hillock at the end of their driveway and continued to mull over the morning's revelations until the radio at his side brought him back.

"Manuel, are you there?"

"Si, senor Edward," he quickly replied.

"What the fuck's going on. I come up onto the bridge here and look over at the gringo's boat and I see that the bitch is back. Where's she been? What's going on?"

Manuel had to think quickly as he wasn't sure he wanted to tell Edward everything. "She went shopping."

"Shopping? Shopping for what? She's been gone three and half hours. How much can you carry on a scooter?"

"Well," Manuel hesitated. "She also went to a meeting of some kind."

"What do mean a meeting of some kind? No wait. Get your ass back here to the boat. I want to talk with you."

"Si, senor," Manuel regretted having said anything. The couple and their kids seemed like OK people to him and he knew how Edward's mind worked. He'd find some way to turn Tory's weakness against her and he was already feeling like he'd broken the sanctity of a confessional by telling Edward about the meeting. Reluctantly he drove to the other side of the harbor where Paulo was waiting for him in the dinghy.

Paulo snickered at him as he boarded. "I think Edward's quite angry with you. You must have done something muy grande to piss him off so. If I were you Manuelito I would tell the man whatever he wants to hear. In case you hadn't noticed he's quite loco over this gringo and his

family, eh? The sooner he has his little revenge we can leave this piss-
hole of an island and make some dinero. So don't fuck about amigo!"

"Don't call me amigo Paulo. I don't befriend cockroaches," Manuel
returned. Paulo only smiled back looking forward to the confrontation
between Manuel and Edward.
      Edward was at the rail as soon as they pulled alongside.
      "Manuel, what the fuck's wrong with you?"
      "Nothing, Senor Edward."
      "Well, what sort of meeting was the woman at? What's the big
secret?"

"It's no secret. I just didn't think it important." Manual knew
firsthand the kind of hurt that Edward was capable of inflicting on others
and took a moment more before answering. On some deep level he knew
that he was at a turning point.

"Manuel, I'm not fucking around, what was the fucking bitch doing
downtown?" Edward was poised over him and he knew he only had a
few more seconds before Edward exploded with rage.
      "She was at an NA meeting," he muttered with downcast eyes.
      "A what? What is that, an automobile club or what?" Edward raged,
now confused.
      Paulo simply smiled and offered, "No, Senor Edward. That is an
organization for the treatment of drug addicts I believe," he watched
Manuel as he imparted this information and was rewarded to see him
cringe.
      "She's a drug addict, and you didn't think I'd be interested?" Edward
screamed.
      "She does not seem like a bad person Senor. I don't see the need in
harming her," Manuel replied.
      "You don't see the need in harming her? Oh this is perfect," Edward
laughed to himself. "Oh yes, perfect! Manuel, let me get this straight,
this lady was once a drug addict and no longer is?"
      "I believe so, Senor Edward."

Edward turned and slapped Manuel hard. "You've worked for me for almost two years so I am not going to kill you, this time. If it was anyone else I would, but if you ever cross me again, lie to me or withhold anything, I will kill you. Understand? Now get out of my sight!"

Manuel went below feeling as though he'd betrayed this woman he hardly knew, but more importantly, that he'd betrayed himself. Before, he'd been naive and perhaps ignorant of the consequences of the trade in which he was engaged. That was no longer the case. He struggled with these thoughts as he went below to his cabin to stay out of Edward's way.

As soon as he was out of sight Edward pulled Paulo aside. "The man and the children are not aboard, correct?"

"Si, Senor. They left about an hour ago. I have seen no sign of them ashore and assume they have gone off with the people who live in the house."

"OK, good. We must act quickly as we don't know when they'll return. Take the dinghy with one other crew and head over to their boat and tell the woman that there has been some kind of an accident and that her husband sent you to bring her across the harbor in our dinghy. Then bring her here. I have a little surprise for her. Do it now!" Although Edward's plan was still forming in his mind he had the basic pain and suffering he wanted to inflict worked out, and would just wing the rest. He hurried below to his cabin to prepare.

Rip Converse

Chapter 12

Tory was hungry when she returned to the boat and went below to the galley to make herself a sandwich. She was just sitting down to eat when she heard the whining, pinging sound of an outboard pulling alongside and then Clifton started barking. She climbed on deck expecting to see Ryan and the children. Instead, she was met by Paulo and one of the other crew off the White Lady. They were hanging onto the side of her boat looking up with agitated looks on their faces. Clifton seemed unusually upset and protective and continued to bark.

"Clifton, stop already!" She'd never seen him act that way before and had to yell at him several more times before he reluctantly backed off some and stopped barking. "I'm sorry, I don't know what's wrong with him this morning. He's usually friendly to everyone. Can I help you?"

"Yes, I think so anyway. Do you live here on this boat with a man and two children?"

"Why yes. Is something wrong?"

"I'm afraid so. The man who lives here on the boat with you asked that we bring you across the harbor as quickly as possible. There has been some type of accident and one of your children has been hurt."

Tory's heart lurched. "Oh my God, which one? What happened?"

"I don't know Senora. I'm very sorry. He just asked us to come and get you as quickly as possible and said only that one of them was hurt."

Tory didn't hesitate even long enough to grab a pair of shoes and jumped down into their dinghy. As soon as she was in, Paulo stole a quick, smug glance at the other crewman and accelerated the dinghy up onto a plane away from Parthenia and back across the harbor. As they sped across the water Tory's mind was so concerned about what may have happened that she didn't even notice that they were not quite headed to the customs pier area and did not suspect anything was amiss until they suddenly veered to starboard and pulled up to the stern of the White Lady.

"Why are you stopping? I thought we were going across to the landing in St. Georges?" she asked, still not yet suspecting anything.

The engineer and another crew quickly stepped out onto the stern platform as they came to a halt. Paulo was anxious to avoid a struggle in broad daylight and smoothly said that he had to get something and would only be a moment. As soon as the lines were affixed, the two crew quickly grabbed her by the arms and rushed her off the platform and through the aft engine room door to get her out of sight as quickly as possible. Tory started to struggle. The watertight doorway into the engine space was sufficiently small that both crew could not stand on either side of her and drag her through and she almost broke free until one of them slammed his fist into the back of her neck several times. Still conscious she continued to struggle as they dragged her into the engine room and one of them finally punched her hard in the stomach and cuffed her sharply on the side of the head with his hand. That ended the struggle.

Tory awoke about 10 minutes later in Edward's opulent cabin, her hands and legs bound with duct tape, lying on his bed. He was sitting in a chair looking calmly down on her when she came around and Paulo was standing at the foot of the bed. She immediately started screaming.

Edward sat passively listening to her for several moments and then casually got out of the chair leaned down and slapped her. "No one can hear you, but it annoys me, so stop, or I will hurt you. Understand?"

Tory sensed that what he said was true and stopped. "What do you want with me? I don't even know you."

"I know. But I know you, and I know the man you live on the boat with. It's not my intention to harm you, I am simply lonely and want someone to party with. I've been watching you for several days and you look like someone who would be fun to party with. That's all."

Tory was confused. "What on earth are you talking about?"

Edward reached over and started to pull her shirt out of her shorts. Tory struggled against the tape that was binding her. He slapped her again several times.

"What? You kidnapped me so that you can rape me? That's insane. You're in the middle of Bermuda harbor on a small island in the middle of the Atlantic. Do you think you'll be hard to find after?"

Edward pulled his chair closer to the bed and again reached for her shirt and pulled it up before answering. As he started his reply, he stared fixedly at her chest and could see her heart fluttering in fear just beneath the skin. He casually ran his hand over her breasts and pinched one of the nipples until Tory flinched.

"Yes, very nice. As I was saying, I'm just a lonely man who is looking for a party companion. I was watching you last night and it seems you have some very healthy appetites. And no, I'm not particularly worried about being caught as I doubt very much that you will say anything to anyone."

"You're crazy. The second I get off this boat I'll report you to the authorities. Now, if you stop right now before it goes any further, I won't say anything. Just take me back to my boat and I will say nothing. You have my word." Tory replied.

"No, I think not. I have a little plan and I don't believe you would keep your word anyway. You seem like far too willful a woman to allow my insult without retribution of some kind. So, as I said before, we will first have a little party and then we will discuss you leaving."

Edward got up from the chair, walked over to the dresser, and folded back the flap on a little kit that he occasionally used on himself. Inside were a syringe and several packs of sterile needles. He made sure that Tory could see what he was doing as he slowly broke the seal on one of the packages and screwed the needle onto the syringe.

Tory was frantic at this point and struggled anew with the tape that bound her wrists behind her back. Did he intend to kill her? Tears started to flow down her face as she struggled with the rope and she started to hyperventilate. All the while Edward ignored her as he made his preparations. After preparing the syringe he opened the top dresser draw and pulled out a baggy of rock cocaine and after opening it and inhaling several breaths of its strong chemical smell sat down again in the chair next to her and held the bag up for her see.

"I understand from my men that you have a strong love for this." He brought it closer to her face so she could see it clearly and again held the bag open, this time close to her nose so that she could smell it.

"Almost pure, Peruvian flake. Nice, eh?"

Tory stopped struggling only because she suspected that he might have something other than killing her in mind. "I still don't understand. Why're you doing this? What have I ever done to you?"

"You, my dear, have done nothing, but the man you live with, is he your husband?"

"No."

"No matter," he continued. "In any case he, bothers me. Let's just say he's inconvenienced me and that's why you're here."

"What are you going to do?" Tory asked.

"Very little. I'm just going to give you one shot and you will do the rest."

"I still don't understand. Ryan annoyed you so you kidnap me and are going to shoot me full of drugs? What will that accomplish?"

"Let's just say I'm an expert of sorts on the effects that drugs can have on the family unit. Quite simply I intend to punish him for his interference through you. If that seems a bit excessive, well, so be it. That's just the type of man I am, excessive. Yes, I like that. Perhaps it would be easier for you to just think of me as a very bad person. My mother always felt that way." Edward got up again and returned to the dresser where he lit a small propane torch. Then he carefully poured a small amount of the coke into a spoon and put it under the propane flame. It quickly melted.

Tory frantically tried to think of anything she could do or say to slow down this impossible chain of events. If anyone had told her an hour ago that she was about to be kidnapped and drugged by an insane madman she would have thought that person crazy. She knew she had little chance of escaping the cabin, let alone the boat, before he carried out the rest of his plan. Her shirt was still pulled up over her breasts and the ugly little man with the bad teeth just stood there at the end of the bed staring at her. She tried squirming back and forth and upwards on the bed in an effort to drag the shirt back down over her chest. As she did so Paulo just smiled and a small bit of saliva drooled out of the side of his mouth.

"Senor Edward, do you think I might enjoy the woman a little bit before we send her back?" he asked.

"I think not Paulo. You tend to play a little rough and I don't want to leave any marks on her, just yet, although I can promise you some time with her daughter if she fails in any way to do what we say."

Tory reacted to his comment like someone had stuck a cattle prod in her side.

"You fuck! I still have no idea what you're doing with me but if you touch either of my children I'll spend the rest of my life looking for you and cut your fucking diseased balls off!"

Edward tsked her. "Such language. And from so small a woman. No matter, I'm almost done here and then you'll be much more civil."

Tory's mind spun as he finished his preparations. Did he really know what he was doing or would he overdose her? Would this reactivate her obsession and compulsion for the drug as he obviously planned? What would Ryan's reaction to the whole thing be?

He finished up and sat back down in the chair at the edge of the bed and she looked over at the needle which he tapped several times as he held it up to the light and then looked down into her eyes.

"Now, this won't hurt a bit. Actually, I'm rather counting on the fact that you'll enjoy it." He took a length of surgical tubing and tied it securely just below her bicep on the arm closest to him. Then he swabbed her arm with a little cotton ball soaked in alcohol as if sterility was a concern, then lay the tip of the needle against the largest of the veins now swollen in the crook of her elbow.

She made one last attempt to get him to stop. "Please don't do this. Do you have any idea what that shit did to me?"

"Not specifically, but I know from one of my men who has been watching you that you used to have a passion for it. Not to worry, there's plenty more where this came from and it's my hope that we will become close friends after."

Throughout his meticulous preparations Tory had watched, on one level, frightened to death, on another, the addict in her had definitely stirred. Just the sight and smell of the quality flake had twitched some little synapse in her medulla oblongata, almost like the feelings of arousal she felt prior to sex. It was totally involuntary and against everything she'd worked so hard for over the previous year, but it had been there none the less, and she hated her body for betraying her.

"Please, I'm begging you, don't do this." A single tear dripped down Tory's cheek.

Edward smiled and slid his answer into her arm. At first she felt only the sting and then like a master he smoothly injected about half the drug, stopped for several moments and then withdrew the plunger drawing some of her blood back into the syringe. Then he waited again. Tory began to feel the wonderful warmth and exhilaration of the drug entering her system. Her eyelids twitched several times from the pleasure. Then Edward booted the rest home.

Tory's whole body rushed. Her head felt like someone had blown the back of it off as the potent drug raced through her system and heightened every sense to a delicious level. At that moment nothing else mattered and she reeled with the pleasure. The levels had shifted, and in that moment the addict in her ruled. The sober, N/A attending, responsible mother was now just a small, shy, voice far back in her consciousness.

"Oh God, what have you done?" she muttered aloud.

"Nothing you didn't want sweets," Edward intoned very pleased with the effects the drug was having on her.

"Paulo, we have very little time left and have yet to reach an understanding with the little lady. Pull her shorts down." He turned back to the bureau for his last surprise.

Paulo smiled, unzipped her shorts and roughly sea-sawed them down to her knees. Tory squirmed against his efforts but this only caused him to be rougher. Her panties still partially covering her, Paulo expertly snapped open his knife and with two quick flicks of his wrist severed the two small waist straps. Then he reached down, tore them up from between her legs, and threw them in the corner.

Edward turned back from the dresser and sat down again on the edge of the bed. In his hand was the stainless-steel shaft of a scalpel that he was holding in his four fingers like a paring knife.

"Please, oh please don't do this. I swear I'll do anything you ask, but don't cut me!" Tory screamed.

Edward slowly brought the blade down to her chest and laid the small blade flat on one of her naked breasts up against her nipple and placed his thumb on the other side. He just let it sit there for several seconds maximizing the terror that Tory was feeling and then he brought the scalpel towards his thumb using the nipple as a fulcrum point. It was as if he was going to cut a bad spot out of an apple. Even the light pressure he exerted caused the blade to penetrate the skin and Tory looked down and cried out in horror as the blade cut partway into her nipple. He stopped the scalpel at that point and reached down between her legs and roughly massaged her labia to imply additional threat.

"Now listen carefully to me. As I'm sure you can feel, I have absolute power over you. I could do whatever I wanted with you right now. I'm sure you can feel that?"

"No, I mean yes, I can!" Tory cried hysterically.

"Good. I want you to remember this well. I'm going to release you in a few moments and it's important that you leave convinced of this power. If you say anything to anyone about our little rendezvous I will take your whole family and slaughter them. I will let Paulo here mutilate your sweet little daughter first and even though I am not a parent myself, I would not wish that on anyone. You see, Paulo is not a well man."

Edward removed his hand from between her legs. "Now, I'm going to have him take cut the tape off your wrists and ankles and I want you to sit up and then straighten your clothes Tory, that's your name, right?" Edward asked. He motioned with his head for Paulo to cut her bindings.

"Yes, that's my name," She replied.

Paulo pushed her over onto her stomach and cut the duct tape around her hands and then then cut the tape on her ankles.

"Sit up."

Tory did as instructed and then hurriedly pulled her shorts up and her top down.

"Here's what we're going to do." Edward reached for the bag of flake next to him and held it out to her. "This is yours. Consider it a gift from me to you. When you leave here you can throw it over the side if you like, but I doubt that will happen. The only thing I ask in exchange for my little present, is that you tell no one of our little meeting. If you say anything to anyone, especially the local authorities I will make sure that your children and your boyfriend are slaughtered. And I mean slaughtered. The children will of course be sexually violated prior to their deaths. It's very important that you understand this and believe it. It will happen, maybe not today or tomorrow, but it will occur. I have the power to make this happen, anywhere. Do you believe this?"

He wanted her to think that he was part of some great system like the Cali Cartel or the mob and even though he did in fact transport indirectly for the cartel, because of previous incidents and his own drug use he was not considered an insider. Instead he was little more than a highly paid truck driver and any request he made to pursue some woman and her children because of imagined slights to him would only be looked on as a further sign of his instability. Tory did not know this though.

She raised her head some and looked him in the eye. "God knows why you did this, but yes, I believe you," she replied.

"Good, very good. Now, Paulo is going to escort you onto deck and take you back to your boat. It's really that simple. We may or may not see each other again, I haven't decided yet."

Edward stuffed the bag of cocaine into her shorts pocket. Paulo opened the cabin door and Tory quickly followed him aft towards the stern.

Edward stood for several minutes in front of the full-length mirror in his cabin smiling at himself and his incredible evil.

"You know Edward sometimes you are so bad you surprise even me," he said to himself. Although he seldom indulged in the needle himself, he decided that this was one of those special times that called for special celebration and bent over the set of works and snapped in a new needle.

Chapter 13

It was not until they were back in the White Lady's Zodiac and speeding across the harbor towards Parthenia that Tory started to breath normally again and believe that there might be some way out of this unbelievable situation. As they pulled alongside, she was relieved to see that Clifton was still the only one aboard. Ryan and the children were still with Mike. She needed time to think. Tory scrambled out of the Zodiac and over Parthenia's rail before Paulo even came to a complete stop and hurried below without once looking back. She felt soiled and violated and even the idea of eye contact with Paulo filled her with revulsion.

End of Part I

Preview of Maelstrom Part II

Chapter 1

As soon as she was below, Tory peeled off her top and examined herself. She gently gathered her damaged nipple between two fingers and bent it downwards in the direction of the cut and started to shudder and sob. Edward's actions had been very calculated and had scared her on a primal level. Her nipple would heal without stitches, but she knew she would go to her grave remembering the moment he'd pinched her nipple between the shiny scalpel blade and his thumb. She sat there for several minutes sobbing quietly, confused not just by the whole incident, but also from the effects of the cocaine. Eventually she pulled herself together enough to realize that if Ryan ever found her like this he would be uncontrollable and demand to know what'd happened. For the time being, she couldn't let that happen. She believed absolutely what the animal on the yacht had said about slaughtering all of them and for the moment her maternal instincts overrode her anger and fear. She quickly gathered her blood-stained top off the floor and buried it at the bottom of the galley trash and then ran into the head where she showered carefully and then applied two Band-Aids across the nipple to stabilize it. She prayed the separated area would reattach itself with time and not become infected. As she dressed in clean clothes and brushed her hair she felt the first effects of the drug wearing off and sat down, overwhelmed at the atrocity committed on her.

'I have to pull myself together!' she thought and reached down to pick her shorts off the floor to throw in the hamper. As she did so she remembered the bag of coke. She sat down again at the salon table and took the baggy out. Inside there was more coke than she'd ever seen in one place at one time and she absently fondled the rocks through the plastic. She wanted things to be as they'd been several hours ago, but the addict in her had other plans and suggested that it was probably a good idea, 'just in case', to hide the cocaine instead of flushing it. Although she didn't at this point plan on using any of it, better safe than sorry and she put it behind one of the bulkheads in the head. The significance of her keeping the coke instead of throwing it out was not lost on her.

Clifton had been laying in the cockpit with his head at the top of the ladder since she'd returned and whined softly in empathy at the sound of her crying. Tory looked up at the sound and climbed the ladder bringing her head level with his. She desperately needed a hug from someone and reached out to the big dog. Clifton seemed to see right into her soul and he licked the tears off her face with unusual gentleness.

"Oh Clifton, I'm not a bad person. Why is this happening to me?" She began crying again. Clifton lay there as she hugged him. The sound of Ryan and the children broke the spell only moments later. Clifton heard them first and lifted his head at the sound of their voices. Following his lead she peeked around the corner of the cabin house and could see them at the float getting into the dinghy and knew she only had a few more minutes to pull herself together and retreated to the head to wash her face again. The shot that Edward had administered earlier was giving way to the crashing depression that always followed the coke high and she was certain that Edward or one of his men was watching the boat. She knew if she went on deck feeling as she did, she would fall apart. With almost no conscious thought of the consequences she grabbed a Bic pen off the salon table and rushed back into the head. Once inside, she opened the cabinet behind the toilet, reached behind the bulkhead and withdrew the coke. Then with a deft skill borne of years of experience, quickly crushed one of the smaller rocks on the countertop with a deodorant can, pulled the ink cartridge out of the pen and then using the empty barrel as a tube, inhaled a large line of the crushed cocaine into each nostril. It was as if only hours instead of years had passed since her last snort and she rocked her head back with the pleasure of the pure coke smacking into the sensitive tissue in the back of her nose. Almost immediately her fear and depression were replaced by the artificial courage and elation of the coke. Now she could face the three of them. She quickly ran a brush through her hair again before facing Ryan and her kids.

"So how did it go?" She asked from the companionway hatch as they pulled alongside. She tried her best to sound nonchalant and normal.

Willy was first to reply. "Oh mom, you should have seen that thing. After we rigged it, Mike took us for a sail and we raced against one of the other ones at the Dinghy Club. There must have been a million square feet of sail on that thing."

"Yeah mom, it was pretty cool. You should have been there," Jan added as if everything Willy said needed to be verified and played down.

Ryan was still tying up the dinghy with his back to her and Tory waited expectantly for him to turn around. If she could just hold it together when their eyes met for the first time, she was sure she'd be all right. Ryan turned. "Hi babe."

Tory looked up at him with the beginnings of a smile on her face, and then her lip started to tremble and she turned away.

Ryan immediately came over, sat down next to her, and put his arm around her. "You OK?"

"Yeah. Why?" she replied keeping her face averted.

He reached over and gently turned her head towards him. "You look sad. Is everything alright?"

'Christ, how could he have noticed so quickly?' she thought to herself. She knew her eyes were still puffy and he was so tuned into her he knew already that something was wrong. "I guess I've just been having kind of a delayed reaction to the whole week in Massachusetts. You know, thinking about Pops. I've been a little sad is all."

Ryan hugged her and pulled her head onto his shoulder. "I know, it's tough. You'll probably have rough days for a while yet. Anything I can do?"

Tory felt a tremendous guilt for the lie she'd just told Ryan. It was her first one and a way of being that she thought she'd left behind forever. "I don't think so, I think I just have to go with it. Thanks for asking though."

"Do we have anything special planned tonight?"

"Not that I can remember?" she replied. "I think I'd just like to hang out though, I don't feel like doing much of anything."

"No problem. Just let me know if there's anything I can do."

"I will."

As the dinner hour approached the cocaine wore off again and Tory found it increasingly difficult to sit still. The high she'd experienced earlier had not provided the same good feelings as her highs of the old days, but the depression and paranoia that followed were everything she remembered, and more. As the afternoon wore on the boat seemed to get smaller and smaller and she started to feel as though everyone was watching her. She couldn't read for more than a few moments at a time, didn't feel like cooking, and whenever one of them engaged her in conversation she'd cut it short because she was sure they'd somehow know that she'd been using. She knew her body language was jumpy and she had trouble looking anyone in the eye. Jan had always been able to tell when she was high and until she figured out what to do, she couldn't bear the thought of any of them knowing that she'd fallen off the wagon. Edward may have introduced the drug into her system, but when she'd gone into the head and had those few lines after, there had been no one standing over her. She could rationalize all she wanted, but bottom line, she blamed herself for the subsequent use.

"Are you cooking tonight, or am I?" Ryan finally asked.

"Would you mind? I really don't feel that well."

"Sure, no problem. Do you want anything in particular?"

Tory felt like she was going to explode from the tension of even this simple conversation and tried to think of some way of escaping. "I don't think so. My stomach's been bothering me all afternoon and I feel kind of punk."

"You want something for your stomach?" Ryan asked.

"Yeah, that's a good idea, but I'll get it. Maybe I just need to sit on the toilet for a while." Tory hurried for the head knowing that the moment she was alone that she would use again to relieve the anxiety. She crossed the cabin quickly and shut the door, grateful for the respite from everyone's imagined scrutiny, quickly reached behind the bulkhead and removed the coke. Then she sat down on the closed toilet and just stared at the bag for almost a full minute. 'After these lines, the rest goes down the toilet,' she told herself firmly. 'I still don't know what I'm going to do, but this shit sure as hell isn't helping.' She took a rock out of the bag and when she heard Ryan getting out the pots and pans in the galley for dinner took advantage of the background noise and crushed the rock and quickly snorted it.

As Ryan cooked, he thought about Tory's behavior all afternoon. She seemed sad about something, but she also seemed unusually nervous and distracted as if something else were troubling her. He was trying to give her the space she obviously wanted to work something out, but when she hurt, he hurt, and decided to bring it up with her later. Whatever it was, there wasn't any reason she should have to go through it alone.

In the head, Tory snorted several more lines and after carefully cleaning up the coke residue off the counter she brushed her hair and returned to the salon, her thoughts of throwing out the coke forgotten. She felt like she could deal again. Anxious to cover her earlier withdrawn behavior she came up behind Ryan and put her arms around him. "I feel a little better now. It must have been something I ate."

Ryan continued to chop vegetables as she spoke, grateful for her touch. "I'm glad you're back. I know you've been kind of distracted all afternoon and I didn't know how much I'd missed you till now. You're touch feels good."

"I'm sorry I've been so distant. You know how important you are to me right?"

"Yeah, I know."

"And that I'd never intentionally hurt you," she continued.

Ryan turned. "Of course, I know that. What do you mean?"

"Nothing. I just wanted to say that." She kissed him warmly.

Tory hardly touched her food but kept it together for the next two hours as the others ate and then got ready for bed. Ryan climbed into Willy's bunk to read him a story and Jan lay in her own bunk, also reading. Tory went up on deck to try and think the whole situation

185

through. She sat in the dark in the cockpit and looked across the water at the White Lady. Although the darkness made her feel less visible to the boat across the harbor, she knew they'd be watching for any signs of movement and the blackness seemed to heighten her increasing sense of isolation and panic. The lines she'd had several hours before had worn off again and she knew she had to think of something to break the cycle that Edward had so cleverly instigated. Her physical compulsion for the drug was like a sleeping giant that had been reawakened. She'd been an addict long enough to know that her use would go on and on until she either ran out of drugs, or something disastrous happened to the four of them. Neither alternative was acceptable. She sat for almost an hour going round and round trying to think of some way out, becoming more depressed as the drug gradually wore off. Finally, with depression overwhelming her she peered down into the main cabin. The only light still on was the one in Willy's bunk where Ryan had fallen asleep reading. Jan's light was out and Tory assumed that she'd also fallen asleep. As quietly as possible she climbed down the companionway ladder. Clifton was at the bottom and groaned softly as she gained the foot, looked up at her and yawned once before putting his head back down and closing his eyes. Tory knew where all the worst creaks in the floorboards were and continued to creep across the cabin, avoiding those areas until she got to the head door. She surveyed the cabin once more and, satisfied that everyone was still asleep, eased the door open, entered and closed it softly behind her. The door was only three quarters of an inch thick, so she kept her movements as quiet as possible, wishing that there was some background noise in the main cabin as there had been earlier, to cover the sounds as she got high again.

Jan was not asleep as Tory had assumed and watched through half closed eyes as Tory crept across the cabin and into the head. Because of her normally quiet nature no one seemed to notice that she too had been quiet all afternoon and she'd just stuffed her suspicions like the old days, afraid to speak and confront, feeling somehow responsible as children often do when bad things happen to their parents. Jan felt like someone was crushing her chest or choking her, because she had suspected, just minutes after returning to the boat, that Tory was high again. She'd spent too many years terrified of Tory's next binge not to be hypersensitive to the slightest change in her mother's behavior and although she wasn't sure what she was high on, she knew there was some poison cursing through her. She felt totally powerless in addition to feeling responsible. What had they all done wrong for Tory to want to use again? In what way had she failed her mom?

She listened intently for the next several minutes hearing occasional movement in the head, and then after a pause, the distinct sound of Tory snorting the lines. It was a sound she knew well and she hugged herself as a tear rolled down her cheek. 'I don't know if I can go through this again,' she thought to herself. 'No matter how I am, how I act, how much I try to help she goes back to it. Maybe she'd be better off if she didn't have the responsibility of me and Willy and maybe she could finally get sober and find some peace.' That's all she thought her mother wanted, peace, from whatever demons drove her. Jan knew she wasn't a bad person and knew that Tory loved them very much, but she also knew how much pain Tory had been over the last few years and she just wanted her to have some happiness. "Yes, maybe she'd be better off without me."

Assuming everyone to still be asleep Tory decided to stay in the head a few minutes longer and have several more lines and didn't hear Jan as she quietly slipped out of her bunk and up onto deck.

Jan stood in the stern for several minutes quietly crying to herself, wishing life weren't so unfair and afraid she would lose her nerve if she waited too long. Finally, she climbed over the stern rail, hung from it, and dropped as quietly as possible into the still, black water.

Below, Tory leaned back against the toilet seat with her head back, reveling in the rush of the almost pure cocaine. Totally into the high she heard nothing as Jan swam slowly off into the dark.

Jan didn't really know how she'd do it but assumed if she swam long enough, eventually she would tire and slip under the water; out of her own pain and able to take some away from Tory. She continued to swim towards the darkest area of the harbor.

Clifton did not stir when Jan crept past him and up the ladder, but when Jan slipped into the water the sound registered in his mind for what it was and he pulled himself to his feet. As their self-appointed guardian he took his responsibility for the two children very seriously. Anything out of the norm got his special attention and the sound of the little girl climbing the stairs into the dark night and going into the water was wrong. Jan was making very little noise as she swam away from the boat, but he continued to concentrate on the diminishing sounds. Following his instinct that all was not as it should be, he tentatively put his front paws on the ladder. Normally Ryan or one of the others would have lifted his hind section at this point to help him the rest of the way up the ladder and he looked expectantly back into the cabin, but no one was there to help. He hesitated a moment more, desperately wanting to get on deck to check on Jan but scared of falling down the stairs. He whined once softly and looked back over the cabin again and realized that he'd have to do it on his own and raised himself as high as possible on his hind legs. His front paws were only two steps from the top of the ladder. He knew he would only have to jump once if he did it just right. He hesitated again for just a second, squatted down several inches on his hind quarters for maximum thrust and jumped, hoping his hind legs would find purchase on the second step that he would need to push him up and over the lip and into the cockpit.

Only one of his hind legs found the step and he almost tumbled back down; the wind knocked out of him from smashing onto the top stair. After a brief struggle he was able to locate the step with his other rear leg and bounded the rest of the way and into the cockpit.

When Clifton stumbled and scrambled up the remaining steps, Ryan woke immediately. He opened his eyes and rubbed the sleep out of them before looking over the cabin. Where were Tory and Jan? He eased himself over the edge of the bunk trying not to wake Willy and walked to the ladder and climbed up, expecting to see Jan and Tory in the cockpit. When he gained the deck his eyes slowly adjusted to the dark and instead of finding Tory and Jan, he saw only Clifton looking intently into the dark night.

"What's wrong boy?" Clifton looked back at him and then back at the water and barked sharply several times. Ryan walked to Clifton's side in the stern and strained his eyes into the night to see if he couldn't see what had upset Clifton so. He noted that their dinghy was still securely tied and off their stern. "Clifton, shush! You're going to wake everyone up."

Below, Tory was also startled out of her drug-induced state at the sound of Clifton bounding up the stairs. Expecting the sound would also wake everyone else, she hurried to hide the cocaine and pen shaft behind the bulkhead before heading out into the cabin. Ryan and Jan were no longer in the cabin and she could hear Clifton barking on deck. As she started up the stairs to see what was going on, she met Ryan who was about to start down.

"Oh, there you are. I heard Clifton and went up on deck and didn't see you or Jan when I got up here. I couldn't figure out where you were," Ryan said.

"What do you mean me or Jan?" Tory looked back into the cabin towards Jan's empty bunk. "She's not up here with you?" A sick feeling started in her stomach.

"No, check the foc'sle bunk."

Tory quickly ran to the bow. "Oh God Ryan, she's not here!" She immediately assumed Edward or one of his crew had somehow taken her.

Clifton started barking again and jumped over the side and started swimming towards the area where he'd last heard swimming sounds.

"Christ, what's going on?" Ryan asked as Clifton jumped over the side.

"They must have taken her!" Tory screamed.

"Who? What? What the hell are you talking about Tory?"

"The men, the men on the boat!"

Ryan had no idea what she was talking about but knew he had to get Clifton back and grabbed the cockpit flashlight and jumped down into the dinghy. As he untied it Tory ran on deck.

"Oh Ryan, it's all my fault. They must have her."

"Tory, get a grip! What the hell are you talking about? What men? What boat?"

Tory just pointed towards the White Lady.

Ryan still couldn't figure out what she was talking about but knew he had to hurry before Clifton became lost in the night. "Tory, wait here, I'll talk with you as soon as I get back. I've got to get Clifton."

"No Ryan. They'll kill you!"

"Look I don't know what's wrong with you or what you're talking about but I have to go now or I'll lose him." He started to row away from Parthenia.

"No Ryan!" she cried after him.

Jan had a two-minute head start on Clifton, but he was a good swimmer and caught up with her about 100 yards from the boat. Jan had heard him earlier when he'd started barking and lost some of her earlier resolve at the sound of his bark. It was so dark and lonely in the water and all at once she was scared and not at all sure she wanted to die. She heard Clifton paddling up behind her just as she was starting to panic and turned as he swam alongside. Years before, when Clifton had been a puppy, he'd scratched Ryan rather badly on the back when the two of them were swimming. Ryan had since taught him not to swim up on top of people and when Clifton reached Jan he started swimming a tight circle around her as he'd been trained. The sight of the big friendly dog was all it took to end her earlier thoughts of suicide and she gratefully grabbed onto his collar with one hand. Clifton immediately turned towards the boat and started swimming back, dragging Jan behind him.

Ryan turned the dinghy in the direction he'd seen Clifton head after he'd jumped over and turned on the small flashlight hoping he hadn't gotten far. 'Christ what a crazy night!' he thought to himself. 'And what the hell was Tory raving about men off the boat taking Jan?' As he rowed he started to wonder if Clifton's jumping over the side had something to do with Jan's disappearance. He himself had once sleepwalked over the side of a boat as a child and started becoming more concerned wondering if the same thing might have happened to Jan.

'But she would have woken up when she hit the water,'" he thought to himself. 'unless she hit her head. Shit!'

Ryan only traveled about 50 yards from Parthenia before picking up their forms in the beam of the flashlight about 25 yards off his starboard side. He angled the dinghy towards them. Jan raised her free arm as his light swept over them and he quickly rowed the remaining distance. He grabbed Jan and lifted her into the dinghy first and then the two of them reached back over the side and hauled Clifton in. As soon as Clifton was safely aboard Ryan reached around and hugged Jan tightly to his chest. "Are you alright sweetie?" Jan just looked up with teary eyes, nodded yes, and hugged him back.

Tory was almost hysterical with relief as they pulled back alongside Parthenia. Ryan passed Jan up and Tory gathered in her arms. "Are you OK baby? They didn't hurt you, did they?"

Jan looked at her mother confused. "Who, Mom? What're you talking about?"

"The men. The men off that boat." She pointed again towards the White Lady.

Ryan lifted Clifton through the lifelines and then followed as Tory pointed to the White Lady across the harbor.

"Tory, she was all alone out there. Why don't we all just go below and see if we can't figure out what in the hell is going on."

Once they got below Tory helped Jan out of her wet T-shirt and bundled her up in a large beach towel and then again hugged her. She'd been convinced that Jan had been taken by the men on the White Lady and swore to herself she would not let either child out of her sight again until all of those men were either in prison or dead. She felt doubly responsible, however, because when Jan had ended up in the water, she should have been there for her, but had instead been in the head getting high.

Ryan sat down on the bunk across the table from the two of them and looked pointedly at Tory. "All right would somebody please explain to me what's going on?"

191

Tory still wasn't sure what to say. So much hinged on her next few words and she did not want to lose their love and trust. For the moment she remained mute and just stared back at Ryan not really knowing how to begin. Ryan waited a few moments and then turned to Jan. "What about you. What are you doing out swimming alone at 11:30 at night?"

Like Tory, Jan was afraid to speak. She didn't want to add to Tory's problems or stand between her and Ryan. She too remained silent.

"For Christ's sake! What's going on? You, you're ranting on about men off a boat across the harbor kidnapping Jan, and she's out taking midnight swims, alone in the dark! Somebody talk to me," Ryan demanded.

Tory had shared many of her darkest secrets while in the treatment center, but nothing she'd ever confided before had the implications and possible immediate effects on her and her family, than what she was about to tell. She searched her mind for the right words to begin, and just couldn't find them. Instead, all the built-up strain and pressure of the last 12 hours spilled out and she burst into sobbing tears.

"I was kidnapped, threatened, shot full of fucking drugs, sexually molested and threatened with all of your deaths if I said a word! That's what's going on."

Ryan didn't know what to say at first. At this point about the only the thing he did believe for sure was that somehow Tory had gotten her hands on some drugs and was in some sort of delirium.

"Tory, why do you think these men would want to hurt you? The whole story seems crazy, I mean we're in Bermuda. If any of what you say just said is true these men will be put away for the rest of their lives! You're not making any sense."

"I know it doesn't make any sense. That's what I'm trying to tell you! That's the scariest part of it all. No one in their right mind would do what these men did. That's the kind of people we're dealing with, they're insane!"

"But what could their motivation be? It's crazy!"

"I know it's crazy, I'm the one who was assaulted and threatened. What Edward said didn't make any sense. When I asked him why, he told me it was because of you, that you had somehow insulted or annoyed him as if that were justification to assault me, drug me and threaten the lives of all of you. You tell me, what did you do to this man?"

Ryan thought back to his only direct contact with the man at the restaurant. It didn't make sense. The only part of the story that rang at all true was that Tory had in fact gotten some type of drugs from the men on the boat. He thought back over her erratic behavior all afternoon and what she was claiming. He knew she was committed to sobriety and for another moment tried to give her the benefit of the doubt. "All right, why don't you start at the beginning."

Even though he was saying the right words, Tory knew he didn't believe her. "Ryan, I can tell you don't believe me. You've known me for months now, been around me day and night, seen me up, and seen me down. I finally have my kids back and I'm in love with you. Why would I endanger all of that to get high again? I have my life back for Christ's sake!"

Ryan hung his head and muttered, "I don't know Tory. That's what addicts do. They fuck up their lives and everyone else's."

Tory was deeply hurt and enraged at the same time. "Ryan, how do you explain this?" She roughly pulled her shirt up over her head, reached behind, unfastened her bra, and held her injured breast out for him and Jan to see. Then she carefully peeled off the Band-Aids and tenderly pressed down the nipple so that the two of them could see where it started to separate from the breast. "He did that! He put a fucking scalpel to my breast and threatened to cut my tits off if I said anything to anyone! Do you think I'd do that to myself?"

Tory's indignation and anger were undeniably genuine to both Ryan and Jan. He knew right away that no woman would ever do something like that to herself and that she was telling the truth. A black fury started to build in him as he tried to comprehend what type of person would do this to Tory and without another word he got up, climbed the ladder into the cockpit and started throwing life-preservers and sails aside as he dug his way down to the box beneath in which his pistol and shotgun were stored.

Tory was too startled to move for several seconds when he rushed onto deck. How could he just leave without saying anything? When she heard him starting to throw things around in the cockpit she got up off the settee and climbed the ladder far enough to see what he was doing.

"What are you doing Ryan?"

"I'm getting my gun! I'm going to kill him!"

"No, you can't! Please stop. We have to talk! You have no idea what he's like, and there are at least five men on that boat! Please Ryan, stop. We have to talk first. No one is angrier than I am about this whole thing but please don't rush off and do anything stupid. There's too much at stake!"

"Tory, this is unbelievable. We can't let someone get away with something like this."

"I know, but please Ryan just come back below so we can talk and figure this thing out."

Ryan stood there seething for several more seconds and then reluctantly went below and listened to the whole incredible series of events that had befallen Tory that afternoon.

Chapter 2

Ryan was disbelieving at first, then angry and ultimately silent as he became convinced of Edward's sociopathic nature. His first inclination was to commit a simple, impetuous act of vengeance, but Tory's fear was legitimate and he soon realized that he was dealing with something very different than a simple schoolyard bully as he got the details of what had happened and what was said to Tory. There were obviously no rules or limits to what this man might do, or how far his power extended. Any action he took would ultimately expose both Tory and the children to further danger, especially if he were unsuccessful. This was underscored to him as he watched Jan's face as she listened to Tory. She was clearly frightened to death of the men on White Lady. Jan's reaction as much as anything else reminded him that this was not just about Tory and him, more importantly, it was also about Willy and Jan's safety.

"Jan, I'm so sorry you had to hear this, but I want you to know that Ryan and I will not let anything happen to you or Willy, no matter what."

Jan spoke with a voice older than her years. "It's not your fault mom and in a way I'm almost glad this happened."

Ryan and Tory looked at each other.

"I thought you'd gone back to the drugs on your own. This way it's not your fault."

"Thanks Jan, that means a lot to me."

Ryan interrupted. "Jan, there's one thing I don't understand that sort of got lost in all of this. What you were doing in the water?"

Jan hung her head. "I don't want to talk about that right now. It's not important anyway." At another time both Ryan and Tory would have pursued the subject further but considering their current situation they didn't press.

"So, what're we going to do?" Ryan asked for the time.

"Well, we've decided that you're *not* going to motor over there with a gun and shoot the prick. There are too many of them and where would that leave us even if you were successful? You'd be arrested by the Bermudians for murder and spend the next 25 years in prison and that would still leave his men for us to deal with. And we're not going to go to the authorities. The whole thing would be too hard to prove, and again, leave us vulnerable to retribution whenever he gets around to it. Can we just run?" Tory asked.

Ryan thought for a few seconds before responding. "I suppose we can, but what's to keep him from following us and attacking us. I think it's even more likely once we leave Bermudian waters. Something tells me that getting you hooked on drugs was not the end of his plan. From what you've told me about him he'll want to somehow know that he's hurt me specifically. To do that he has to be close to us. I think he'll definitely follow us if we try and run."

"Is there anything we could do to his boat to keep that from happening, you know, so that at least we could get a head start?" Tory asked.

Ryan thought hard about it for several minutes. "I think I have an idea."

End of Preview Part II

Mailing List

If you would like to join my mailing list please send me an email at ripconverse@gmail.com with the word "add" in the subject line. I promise not to abuse your email address or share it with anyone else; period. I will occasionally use it to let you know about new releases, sales and occasional giveaways.

Reviews

Please leave a review of Maelstrom on Amazon if you enjoyed it. I can't tell you how important reviews are to a new author. They really help other readers find my work and increase my standing. If I can't find readers, I don't make any doe ray me and can't afford to continue writing and improving my work. I loved writing this book and hope to write many more. Thank you for taking the time to read this story. If you have questions or comments, please send me an email at ripconverse@gmail.com. I try to respond to all queries. Your feedback is important to me; both positive and negative. It's how I improve! If you have an interest in receiving an early release of Part II or Part III of this series at no charge in exchange for submitting an early review please email me also. In the subject line put "early review". This offer is only available to the first 15 people who respond.

About Me

I've been a pilot, a boat builder, a cabinetmaker, an investment banker, a publisher, a management consultant, and an accomplished builder of custom, sculpted, rocking chairs (see parkerconverse.com). Over the past 18 years I've built over 150 chairs out of exquisite figured hardwoods. Each one is unique, and custom made.

Of all the things I've done and do, perhaps my favorite is Captain. I've lived on or near the water my entire life and had my first boat at the age of 9. Over the years I've had the good fortune to have sailed in the

Mediterranean, parts of the South Pacific and up and down the East Coast of the U.S. I've also made over 20 offshore passages between New England, Bermuda and the Caribbean and lived aboard a boat in the Caribbean. I worked as a charter captain in the Keys for many years and also worked as a Captain in the oil fields in the Gulf of Mexico. I love the ocean and the skills it takes to be a good Captain and I've accrued over 3,000 incident free days at sea.

For More Information

WWW.RipConverse.com

Instagram.png   Facebook.png   Twitter.png

Made in the USA
Columbia, SC
27 April 2020